Will Hallam
Veer 2 Venus

TRACEY DICKSON

Will Hallam Website
www.willhallam.com

Follow Will on Facebook
www.facebook.com/will2hallam

Will Hallam – Veer 2 Venus

By Tracey Dickson

ISBN: 978-0-9874067-3-6

To My Darling Brother William

A few years on and
I miss you every day
Your absence is noted,
what more can I say
This is the second novel,
to make you a star
Keep guiding me,
don't ever be far.

GLOSSARY OF TERMS

Nicmittee = Committee
Nicmunity - Community
Nicbeings = Beings that live on Venus
Famnic = Family
Great Great Grandnic = Great Great Grandfather
Grand Aquanic = Grandson
Paanic = Father
Maanic - Mother
Bronic - Brother
Sisnic - Sister
Kidnic – Child/Children
Scaleaquanic – Male with scale on his back
Spoutaquanic – Male with a spout on his back
Scalelibnic – Female with scale on her back
Spoutlibnic - Female with a spout on her back
Vennis – Tennis
Vacket – Racket
Vall - Ball

PLANET MERCURY

Tronbeings – The race of aliens on Planet Mercury
Tronmunity – The community of Tronbeings
Maatron – Mother on Planet Mercury
Paatron – Father on Planet Mercury
Brotron – Brother on Planet Mercury
Sistron – Sister on Planet Mercury
Ironkidcaptron – Iron-made boy from Mercury
Rockkidgemtron – Rock-made girl from Mercury
Unctron – Uncle from Planet Mercury

CHAPTER ONE
RETURN

'Ames, I'm so glad you and Pat could come along to this exhibition with me.'

Amy shrugged. 'It's because of you I'm hooked on this space and science stuff anyway.'

'Handy since this exhibition has plenty of both.'

'I see you've got your wristband and your magnifier! Expecting another adventure?'

'I wish!' Will laughed. 'Hey, they're here if something comes up. Let's have a look at what they're doing.'

Will, Amy and Pat headed to a stand where others had gathered, and pushed their way to the front.

'Who wants to ride a geyser?' asked the compere.

Will put up his hand. Amy didn't move so he grabbed her arm and shot it into the air.

'What's a geyser?' asked Amy.

'It's a hot spring that periodically erupts, throwing water into the air. Look behind where the compere is standing. There's a picture.'

'Oh.'

Will felt his face was about to burst if he didn't get noticed shortly.

'What about you, son? You look keen. Do you have any friends with you? We have three spots today.'

'Come on Ames, this will be awesome,' Will said as he grabbed her hand again.

'Let's take Pat with us,' said Amy. 'He said he has three spots.'

1

Will, Amy and Pat ran to the stairs up to the stage and the crowd roared with laughter.

'You've got your dog with you?'

'Yes, and don't worry; Pat will be fine. He'll do everything we do.'

'Pat,' the compere announced, 'Pat the dog, ladies and gentlemen. Let's welcome Pat the dog to the stage.'

There were fits of laughter as everyone was entertained.

'So, son what's your name?' asked the compere as he held the microphone to Will's mouth.

'I'm Will and I love geysers.'

The crowd and the compere laughed. 'That's what we love; an enthusiastic kid. Now what about you? What's your name?'

'I'm Amy and up until a second ago I didn't even know what a geyser was.'

The crowd again roared.

'Something else we love; honesty. All right Will, Amy and Pat, today you're going to ride a geyser.'

Pat barked and the crowd clapped as the compere encouraged Will and Amy to bow at the audience for the beginning of their performance. He then led them to the side of the stage and gave them instructions until they went backstage.

'Ladies and gentlemen, our three stars are getting ready out back, but just as a warning for all you fans at the front, you may get wet.'

The compere looked around and welcomed Will, Amy and Pat as they rolled themselves onto the stage. They were inside individual clear balls large enough that they were able to stand up. The ball moved when they walked in the direction they were headed. The compere indicated the marks on the stage where he wanted them.

Hearing was more difficult inside the balls but the compere spoke loudly to compensate.

'Ladies and gentlemen, here's how this works. Our three stars are positioned correctly. When the geyser erupts it will shoot them straight up, then it is their job to keep walking or running inside their ball to stay on the geyser. The faster they run the higher the geyser lifts them.'

Will was so excited his eyes darted around and this was one adventure Amy embraced. Pat was his usual cool self.

'Ready on the count of three.'

The trio waited.

'One, two, three.'

Three individual geyser fountains spurted out and elevated Will, Amy and Pat toward the ceiling.

They ran like crazy as fast as their legs would take them and sure enough the farther they ran, the farther they were elevated. The thrill was so intense the kids giggled until tears ran from their eyes. At one stage and unintentionally all three looked up toward the bright lights of the exhibition centre just as three bolts of light hit Will's wristband, Amy's headband and Pat's dog collar at the same time, causing them to land on their backsides. They tumbled many times in their clear balls as the room turned pitch black and deafening sounds filled their ears. Finally they were released.

'That would have to be one of the coolest things I've ever done.'

'It was fantastic Will; I loved it.'

'Thanks Will it was certainly up there with a best ever for me.'

'Pat, you're speaking again! How wonderful,' said Amy as she hugged him.

'Ah, guys, it looks like we have company.'

Amy and Pat walked towards where Will was pointing and soon found themselves standing beside a familiar-looking spaceship. It was like the one they'd travelled on before but this one had "CHAMJAN" emblazoned down each side in large black letters.

'I'm CHAMJAN, the female version of the CHAMJET,' it announced.

'The CHAMJET comes in male and female form?'

'Indeed it does, Amy.'

'How do you know my name?'

'I know all your names. CHAMJAN makes it her business to know everything. Unlike CHAMJET, I ask a lot of questions.'

Will was mesmerized by the alluring voice of CHAMJAN.

'Cyril sent me to gather all three of you.'

'How many of you Cham spaceships are there?'

'At this stage just two, Will. Who knows how many Cyril will have in the future.' She waited a moment. 'Why are you all standing there? It's not your first time seeing a spaceship like me. My name is different, and my features are different, the most obvious being I am magenta pink, not aqua blue. I still have the trademark of the shiny silver nose.'

Will looked at Amy then at Pat with a strange expression and CHAMJAN noticed.

'What's up Will?'

'I expected our old buddy CHAMJET.'

'Well you've got your new buddy now. It's horses for courses and I've been sent. You know your seats; we're in a hurry, so hop in.'

'A hurry? What's so urgent?'

'Will, haven't you learnt anything about the way Cyril works?'

'Yes but—'

Will was interrupted as CHAMJAN cut in, 'Cyril is frantic between warming the atmosphere and shedding light. He often thinks he has done something but then remembers he hasn't.'

Will chimed in, 'Why have a last minute if you can't use it?'

'Whatever works!'

'Amy, it does work for him but it makes it damn hard for the rest of us who don't work that way and need to plan.'

'Excuse me Miss CHAMJAN, where are we going?' asked Pat.

'You know the drum. I can't tell you everything... not that I know anything, but nonetheless Cyril will advise all when we get there. Time is moving on; have you got everything?'

'Ames, have you got your headband?'

'Yep, but it's a little tight; I must have more brains now,' she said as she adjusted it and giggled to herself.

Will rolled his eyes as he noticed a shimmer on her finger. 'What's that?'

'It's my crystal ring,' she replied as she proudly displayed it to him.

'And what a priceless purple gem it is,' he mocked.

'Priceless, most likely, a gem, definitely,' she responded smugly.

'Seriously Ames, what's so good about it?'

'It may not look priceless to you Will, but it reminds me of a semi-precious gem called an amethyst. It is believed the stone protects its owner from drunkenness and prevents intoxication.'

Will shrieked with laughter. 'It's wasted on you, as you're too young to drink.'

'When I wear this ring and start to get nervous about things, I hold my finger up and stare at all the different dimensions in it and I don't know why but it calms me down. I call it my ring of calmness.'

Will scrunched up his face. 'Chicks are strange creatures.'

'That's why I never showed it to you before,' said Amy. 'I knew you'd be like this.'

Pat was interested in Will and Amy's banter. 'I didn't know you knew so much about amethysts,' he said to Amy.

'I've only read a little bit about them.'

'So, share your knowledge.'

'This may not be 100% correct but it's my interpretation. When small cavities form inside a rock they're known as geodes. A cavity is basically an air bubble caught inside a rock. How the air gets caught there only nature knows. Once it's there amethyst crystals form and line the inside wall.'

'That's actually really interesting Ames. Where are these rocks found?'

'That's a shock Will,' said Amy. 'I didn't think this would interest you at all.'

'Why not? It's science.'

'I suppose so. The rocks are generally found anywhere there is or was lava close to the surface.'

'That info might come in handy,' said Will.

Pat heard CHAMJAN hissing.

'What about you Will, have you got the magnifier?'

'Check Pat, I've got it right here.'

'And the wristband?'

'Also on board,' he said as he waved his left arm. 'And I see the collar is still around your neck Pat.'

'Yes and just to let you know, CHAMJAN, I've got my singing voice should I need it,' added Pat and he sang a high pitched note.

Bolts of electricity hit the jet, jerking the take off. The star-filled sky lit up with brilliant colours that radiated from the residue from the electricity bolts. Warm orange to cool blue and sizzling reds all mixed together, bouncing off each other, creating an amazing light show. Sadly the passengers were unable to enjoy the light show due to the extreme motion. Amy's face was white as she turned to Will to see if he was okay.

'Amy, you look terrible.'

'I feel rotten and am about to be sick,' she said as she rested her head on the back of Pat's seat.

'Have a look in the drawer,' CHAMJAN announced.

Amy looked down to see a drawer had popped out. It contained an odd shaped purple rock.

'Eat it,' screamed CHAMJAN, 'eat it.'

Amy grabbed the rock and shoved it in her mouth. She was feeling so ill she was not sure at all what it tasted like. A few moments went by and the colour returned to her face.

'What does it taste like?' asked Will.

'I'm not quite sure but I think it's a combination of all my favourites together.'

'The electric storm hasn't ceased so maybe I should play the sick card if that's what you get. CHAMJAN, what are those things called that you gave Amy?'

'Ven-la-roc.'

'How can I get one?'

'You won't need one,' interrupted Pat. 'Look ahead.'

The electric storm passed as did the iridescent array of colours in the sky. The CHAMJAN turned and entered into thick white smoke.

'I can't see anything; not even the back of Amy's head and she's just in front of me.'

'You're not the only one,' said Pat. 'I'm in the front seat and can't see where we're going.'

'This surrounding smoke is different from normal smoke,' said Amy. 'It's so much easier to breathe and I'm not coughing.'

'You're actually surrounded by steam, not smoke. It's the same effect as the steam you get when taking a hot shower,' announced CHAMJAN.

'CHAMJAN, is there any chance steam is our air survival element instead of bubbles this time?'

'I can't answer that Pat as I don't know, but here's how it works. The steam on this low level is ordinary; you can survive on it but after a period of time you will become dehydrated and may even experience a shortness of breath.'

All three listened intently as CHAMJAN guided the jet upwards.

'Up here the steam is lighter, it's easier to breath and this steam will rehydrate and replenish energy. Remember, when you are dehydrated you feel tired and sluggish.'

'Well I don't know about the rest of you but I feel wonderful,' said Amy.

'That's because you've still got the taste of the ven-la-roc in your mouth.'

Amy shot Will a disapproving look.

'You're not going to get over that, are you Will?'

'Damn right CHAMJAN. Not until I get to try one.'

'Look down, Will.'

'Beauty, my very own ven-la-roc, thank you. Now I'll be able to give my expert opinion.'

'Will, now is not the time to shove it into your gob. You need to exercise self-control. In fact you all got one, and hold onto them, because you'll need them.'

Will slid the edible rock into his front pocket for safekeeping, and Amy did the same then assisted with hanging Pat's on his collar.

'Ahhhh, back to the steam, I'm keen to know more about it,' said Pat.

'There's no more to tell than lower dehydrate, upper hydrate.'

'CHAMJAN.'

'Yes Will.'

'If Amy is feeling so wonderful,' he said as he held his fingers up displaying inverted commas with his first two fingers on each hand, 'the ven-la-roc must have some link to that.'

'Right, well thought out.'

Pat sat back, very impressed with Will's question, while Amy marvelled at the steam.

'Although I don't know which planet you will end up on and I don't know Cyril's plans for you, it's important you remember the lower and upper levels of steam,' continued CHAMJAN.

'Is there a name for this steam?'

'Pat, it's an obvious name, survival steam.'

Will scratched his head. 'Wait up CHAMJAN, can you give an example of the distance between the lower and upper level of the steam?'

'It's hard to say, but on a relatively tall mountain maybe half way up or if you think of a lighthouse about half way up also.'

'You mean the same sort of lighthouse that guides ships to safety during the night?'

'Precisely.'

Amy finally tuned back to the conversation. 'How can we tell when we're in the upper level of survival steam?'

'You'll work it out Amy. I've given two really good clues.'

Will was not comfortable with the lack of detail CHAMJAN had released, but Pat noted the tip about the tall mountain and the lighthouse.

'CHAMJAN.'

'Yes, Will.'

'Is there something in those ven-la-rocs that is connected with the different levels of survival steam or that assists with hydration and energy or something else I can't think of right now? Like what if we're unable to get to the upper level?'

'He's not as dumb as he looks, folks,' was all CHAMJAN replied.

After that last comment Pat believed CHAMJAN knew way more than she was sharing with them.

Will had the same inkling. 'Any other clues you want to share CHAMJAN?' Will asked persuasively so CHAMJAN felt compelled to answer.

'Just one more clue; this fights against you.'

CHAPTER TWO
UNEXPECTED NEWS

CHAMJAN gunned the jet, pushing to unimaginable speeds, making their eyes water and forcing the skin on their faces to pull downwards so they looked like freak show performers. The jet darted around and came to a stop as the weightless floating feeling drew them into the atmosphere. A pink puff of smoke nestled a small bottle around each of their necks as a streak of sunlight blinded their view.

'I wonder what that means exactly; "this fights against you." Does it mean it's against me, Will Hallam, on my lonesome or is it against you two as well?'

'I don't know Will but I guess we're about to find out,' answered Amy as she hinted they had company.

Amy was scared but was determined not to show the fear to the others.

'You're finally here!' said an unseen being in a familiar voice.

'Cyril, is that you?'

'It's me.'

The light was blinding and the heat was stifling.

'Wait a minute Cyril, and we'll be able to see you shortly,' insisted Pat.

'I've waited for too long and have left this to the last minute. I believe you already know about me and the last minute?'

'Hmmmm,' noted Pat.

'You won't be able to see me as clearly as last time, because I've increased the strength of my rays to disguise us all. We can't spend a lot of time talking so listen up.'

'Disguise us from whom?'

'The planets, Amy. I don't want them to know we're talking or that you're even here.'

'Why?'

'I need your help, and they'll want to know who you are.'

'Why?'

'The word has spread that the magnifier's been found or at least that it exists.'

'Who told?'

'Hush with all the questions Will and let me be specific. One of the planets in particular has heard that the magnifier exists. She's hot and the tension on her planet is uncontrollable which has forced me to call you.'

Pat assumed his guardian role for the safety of Will and Amy. 'Cyril, it baffles me. Surely, with all your power, you should be able to tell your planets what to do.'

'Pat, are you questioning me on my ability to do my job?'

Pat knew he had to back down fast as Cyril was defensive. 'I just thought you would have more control.'

'I do have control.' Cyril threw his hand to the air and a large bolt of thunder struck.

'There's no need to go to those lengths. I get it.'

'I thought you'd see it my way Pat,' replied Cyril as his rays dulled. He seemed to be shaking. 'Not only do I have control but my planets know more about each other than you may realise.'

'In what way?'

'They know about things like water, air, heat and frozen areas even if those things don't exist on their planet.'

Will observed the situation and thought of a way to smooth it over. 'Here's the magnifier, Cyril. You take it.'

Amy was offended at Will's offering so she whispered to him, 'What are you doing? I gave that to you.'

'Sorry Ames, but there's already tension and we haven't even started,' he whispered back.

'Calm down all three of you. Even if I took the magnifier, and don't get me wrong; I'd like to, Will is the only one with the right hands.'

'But he can't manage alone.'

'That's where you and Amy come in.'

Amy's stomach was in knots, so she calmed herself by peering through her ring.

'Will,' she whispered, 'whatever happens I'm with you.'

'Thanks Ames, I really appreciate it.'

Will nervously ran his fingers through his hair as he cleared his throat. 'Cyril, before we get to exactly which planet can I ask why?'

'Last time you were here your team against the odds completed the task of restoring peace to Mercury.'

'That's because when there's a Will there's a way,' interrupted Will but Cyril was not perturbed, he simply continued.

'Teams before you had taken on the task but failed. You were the first to find Zola and use it as a source to give the gift of air to Mercury. Guess I've got to be grateful for that. Sometimes when you create peace in one area it causes turmoil in another.'

'And Cyril, sometimes when you create peace in one area it overflows to another.'

Cyril soured his face back at Amy as Pat moved on with the questions. 'Are the tronbeings objecting?'

'Yes and no. I know Mercury told you that all planets have tronbeings but that's not necessarily true. It goes much deeper. Will made a pact many years ago. Do you remember, Will?'

'Of course... with my old friend Zac when we were younger.'

'It was then that you were chosen for this battle.'

'You're saying a pact I made with a friend when I was younger is now all these years later going to come back to haunt me?'

'TILOAPS Will, TILOAPS. You need to prove it and/or preserve it. I know preserving it was not part of the initial agreement but it is now. Here's the best part; I can add to that pact whenever I want,' said Cyril smugly.

'So let me get this straight, Cyril, you not only control the universe but are trying to control me as well?'

'Absolutely, Will,' he responded.

Will froze with outrage.

'Cyril, for goodness sake what is TILOAPS?' asked Pat.

'I'm not at liberty to tell you. That is completely up to Will. However should he tell you prior to the right time the contract will be void and harm will come to all three of you.'

'I didn't sign up for this,' said Amy.

'You're signed by association. There's no real contract on a piece of paper as such but you became part of this when you gave the magnifier to Will. And may I remind you that you have property that belongs to me.'

'I don't have anything of yours!'

'Yes you do, and think about it, because I want it back.'

Pat got a premonition that Cyril was now working against them although he had no idea why. 'So we're all bound?'

'Yes Pat you are, one in all in. That's the advantage right?'

'Right I guess if choice is not an option,' Pat murmured back.

Will only half listened to the conversation. He took a deep breath as he heard his father's voice in his head;

'*Be fearless; your greatest fears in life will be the ones you'll have to face.*'

He was grateful for his dad's advice as he squared his shoulders and looked directly at Cyril whose rays had dimmed so his expression was clearer. 'You've pre-warned us that one particular planet is hot and the tension is uncontrollable and ultimately if I reveal the meaning of a pact harm will come to us. So what's to stop us from getting out now?'

'You can't.'

'Why not?'

'Oh dear your human minds... how quickly you forget:

'Point One: CHAMJAN or CHAMJET will not return until your mission is complete.

'Point Two: Now you have completed your first task here you're bound to continue working for me like it or not.

'Point Three: This is by far the most important. Should you choose not to continue, harm will come to you. I am using the word harm mildly.'

A sudden rush of blood filled Will's face as fear encapsulated him.

Pat noticed Will was struggling. 'Okay, okay, so at this moment there's one really angry planet?' he said.

'Yep.'

'And the anger is a result of creating peace on Mercury?' put in Will.

'Not really, Will.'

'I guess the fact I possess the magnifier is no assistance,' Will murmured to himself as he looked down at it.

'Right again; that makes you a very powerful young man Will.' Cyril had heard him.

'Power's one thing I guess, but it's what I do with it.'

'Wise as well,' added Cyril.

'I need an honest answer Cyril.'

'What is it Pat?'

'Are you assisting us or hindering us on this mission?'

'Of course, thanks for reminding me Pat... I've not yet given you your mission. You must generate the Ring of Calmness.'

Amy smirked. She couldn't believe the name she gave to her ring would be their mission.

Pat on the other hand was getting angry. 'I repeat, Cyril, are you assisting us or hindering us on this mission?'

'You'll find out.'

'You're suggesting we take instructions from you but you're not necessarily on our side?'

'The fact is all three of you are too wise and you're smart, you use your strength as a team. I felt sure Mercury would bring you down but it didn't, so let's see how good you are at "generating" this time round.'

'Any further clues as to how we would generate the Ring of Calmness?' asked Amy.

'It's simple. If you can remember the first seven letters of the alphabet, you'll remember your mission.'

'You mean A, B, C, D, E, F and G?'

'Yes, and here is what they stand for:

A, you must Assemble something

B, you must Blast something

C, you must Construct something

D, you must Discover an additional function of something one of you already has.'

'Which one of us already has it?'

'Amy, you'd be the best person to work that out.'

Amy figured he was speaking about her but she had no idea what he was referring to.

Cyril continued.

E, you must Expose something

F, you must Find something

G, you already know, it's Generate the Ring of Calmness.

'Do we have to do all those things in that order?' asked Pat.

'Clues will probably be found out of order but you will work out you need the last one to do the next one.'

'That mission will take a lifetime.'

'Not necessarily Pat. The answers will show themselves to you; the question is whether you recognise them.'

'How will we know if we've got the right thing?' asked Will.

'Your magnifier will not let you down.'

'How will we remember the list?'

'Will, you have a wristband and a magnifier, Amy has a headband and Pat has a collar. What more could you need?'

A hissing noise consumed the atmosphere as three fireballs lit the sky and shot out from behind Cyril directly at Will, Amy and Pat.

'Move aside,' screamed Cyril as the trio hastened out of the way.

'What was that?'

'Judging from the left over residue Amy, it looks like burning lava.'

'Who'd throw lava balls at us? If they'd hit, we would have caught on fire.'

'Not likely. The embers or fireballs which these are that fly out of lava are purely decorative and do not directly cause fires. In my humble canine option it was a scare tactic to send us away.'

'So much for no one knowing we're here,' retorted Amy.

'That's my cue to get out of here. Folks I have to go.'

'Of course you do,' added Amy sarcastically.

'But Cyril—'

'There's no time Will, I've left you the lavalorries.'

'What?'

'The lavalorries, oh and further clues are "magnified" at the date wall.'

Will turned to see three objects behind where he was standing as he pointed. 'How do they work, and what's the date wall?'

The rays of sunlight blinded then faded as Cyril disappeared.

Pat snarled. *We'll show you Cyril; you may be the most powerful object here but power houses have been broken down in the past.*

Will, confused and angry, put his hand up to his forehead.

Amy looked over at him and sighed. 'Come on Will. We can do this.'

'We don't have much choice; we've got to give it our best shot.'

'Well done kids, that's the attitude. Now what have we got?'

'We need survival steam to keep hydrated.'

'Yes Amy, and that's a clue in itself.'

Amy and Will stared at Pat.

'Do I have to tell you everything?'

They continued to stare.

'We must be going to a hot planet!'

'Wouldn't the intense heat we're surrounded in give that away?'

'Not necessarily Will but you know half the planets are terrestrial and—'

Amy cut in. 'We get it, we've been to Mercury, we've just left Earth so it has to be out of Venus and Mars.'

Will had moved over to the lavalorries and Amy stood there with hands on her hips.

'Terrestrial planet number two here we come.'

CHAPTER THREE
UNEXPECTED GUESTS

Pat walked over to the burning embers and put his nose close. He was forced to keep a considerable distance as there was immense heat radiating from them.

Amy watched on. 'Pat what are you trying to prove?'

'I'm seeing if this burning lava has any clues.'

'Good thinking, so what have you come up with?'

'Absolutely nothing! My nose hasn't changed colour and there is no distinct smell to help me out either.'

Will was obsessed with the lavalorries. 'The creations up here are unbelievable; first the anyshapecarts and now the lavalorries. The only problem is the lavalorry is so hot we'll sizzle sitting on one.'

'Steady up Will, we'll work them out. Let's all work at it, then we'll need to go over what we know.'

'Good plan Pat.'

Will, Amy and Pat circled the lavalorries searching for clues on how to cool them down. They had no luck, but after a while Pat decided his collar may have the answer. He jumped to make it spring to life but had no luck. Amy tried her crystal ring by holding the bauble on the end, but no message was reflected. Meanwhile, Will was searching under the lorry for clues through the magnifier.

'Will, anything?'

'Nothing Pat.'

'Stop for a sec,' suggested Pat. 'We've got some clues and we've not considered them. Think outside the square. Rule one, answers or clues are never in obvious places. So what do we know so far?'

'We know the planet is a she, and we've narrowed it down to two options.'

'Yep. What else?'

'She's obviously angry and reacting by throwing burning lava at us.'

'And that, Will, should be the most obvious clue.'

'Do you know the answer?'

'No. I no longer listen to your space projects, so you two work it out.'

'OMG, it's obviously Venus.'

'Explain how you came to that conclusion Will?'

'Lava. Venus has more volcanos on her than any of the other planets, but according to what we've learnt none is active so the lava should be solid, not burning.'

'That may be true of what you've learnt but up here there is a whole new set of rules. Can either of you think of anything else?'

'Her surface is obscured by a thick blanket of cloud,' said Amy.

'Ames is right. The steam we travelled through to get here is a symbol of the clouds.'

'I know another fact about Venus,' went on Amy. 'It's the hottest planet because the cloud cover traps all the heat from the sun so the heat is magnified.'

'My fur might singe.'

'Could do Pat.'

Will remembered more. 'Venus is Earth's twin based on size and it's the only planet that rotates clockwise around the sun. It's often referred to as going backwards. All the other planets go the same way.'

'I'm so proud of you two. I had no idea that Venus is home to so many volcanoes.' Pat looked at the lavalorries. 'We need to get these things working.'

'I'm trying, Pat.'

Pat put his paw out and felt the immense heat emanating from them. 'It's obvious they're too hot to ride in.'

Will used his magnifier to carefully scrutinise every square centimetre, fishing for clues. 'Finally!
Come over here and let's work out mine first, then we'll look at yours.'

Pat and Amy gathered as Will pointed the magnifier at the dash.

'Look at this temperature gauge lever handle. It controls the temperature of the lava these lorries are made of. If the lever's up it's hot and down it's cold.'

'Got that part Will, but what about the in between settings?'

'Not sure yet.'

'Get on with it, switch the setting to cold but make sure the handle's not hot,' instructed Pat.

Will held the magnifier in one hand and pulled the handle down with the other. Instantly the lorry cooled as it changed colour from red/orange to a blue/purple. The colours pulsated throughout the lorry intermittently.

'They only fit one person or in Pat's case one dog at a time,' said Amy. 'What if we need to travel together?'

'There should be a setting for that.' Will used the magnifier again and found two pull handles located on the top back. He slid his fingers around the handles and braced himself to pull in hope it would extend. 'Okay, here goes.' He used all his strength to pull but nothing happened. 'That clearly didn't work. I wonder what I did wrong?'

'Here, let me have a look,' demanded Amy as she snatched the magnifier.

'Careful Ames; we all know the grip the magnifier prefers is not yours.'

'I'm only looking. Surely that can't cause harm.'

Pat sniffed around observing the pull handles. 'This is annoying me, why can't I work it out?'

'Slow down. I know you want to sort this now, but give yourself a moment to work it out.'

'Usually I'm a genius at mastering this stuff.'

'Okay genius, from my observation you've missed something in your haste.'

'What?'

'These things aren't called lavalorries for nothing.'

'Got it, I need to think about the characteristics of lava. It's staring me in the face. I'm trying to reshape a solid object.'

'Right on.'

Will took the magnifier back from Amy. 'Lava needs to be in liquid form to be able to change shape,' he explained. 'And I'm trying to get it to change shape while it's in solid form.'

'Of course! Why didn't I think of that!'

'Cause you didn't, Ames. Thank Pat for the tip,' said Will as he pointed his finger to his nose.

'I'm here to intervene when needed.'

'You know my motto Pat, fake it till you make it. Cyril lives by his saying, and so do I.'

Amy shrugged as Pat lifted his paw demanding that Will concentrate on one thing at a time.

Will pointed the magnifier at the temperature lever and changed the setting from cold back to hot. He returned to the rear and pulled so hard at the two handles, his lavalorry extended right out, allowing for a

back seat. The farther it went out the higher it rose off
the ground. There were no doors; access and egress was
by climbing over the sides, like getting into an army
truck with no doors and no roof but just a frame on top
to hold onto. Will was stoked he'd finally gotten one
thing he really wanted; an open top oversized army tank
version of a lavalorry with room for many, that was high
off the ground and able to ride over anything. A rope
had fallen from the driver's side with a small clearing
path up one side of the lorry that was solid and had
cooled to allow him to climb up the rope and switch the
setting to cool. He stayed up there looking out over the
universe as though he was the king.

'What about the rest of us?' asked Amy.

'Can't you two work yours out?'

'Get over yourself and come and sort mine out for
me.'

'Okay Ames, I'm on my way.'

'If I'd known it was going to be that easy I would've
ordered him around way more,' Amy whispered to Pat.

'I heard that Amy, so don't push your luck. You do
your share of order giving,' said Will as he jumped down
out of his lorry. 'Okay, so you should be able to alter
your own with the use of that priceless gem on your
finger or your headband.'

Pat saw how Will altered his lorry so tried his own
by activating his collar. 'Amy, I think you and I need to
swap. This one's not working for me.'

'Neither is mine,' responded Amy.

Pat hurried to the one Amy had and swirled his
collar around until the hot/cold handle appeared. He
put his paw up and pushed the handle to cold then
instantly the colour changed and so did the temperature.

'Excellent, I'm here and ready to go in my lorry set for one.'

'Do you want any assistance with structural change Pat?'

'No thank you Will. A one human/pet option is ideal for me. I'll be able to travel around without being noticed.' Pat wasted no time jumping in.

Amy held her ring up but nothing happened.

'What's the matter with your ring?' asked Will.

'I don't know.'

'Are there any adjustments on that thing? Does it turn or open or something?'

'Why didn't I think of that?'

Will rolled his eyes as Amy turned the large crystal on her ring and it instantly let out a ray of light.

'It's got some of the same features as my headband,' said Amy. 'Look, it's reflecting my hot/cold handle.'

'Good. Now I've chosen the mega lorry, Pat has the shopping trolley so what do you want?'

'The sleek sports version of course.'

'Course you do. Come around the back here and let me show you. What you get depends on how far you pull the handles out. You have a go so you know what to do.'

Amy grabbed the handles and gave a pull, extending the lorry out a short distance. 'This is so cool; my very own sports lorry! It's not a car, but it'll do.'

'How noble of you Amy, you don't want much and you're not old enough to drive.'

Amy giggled at Pat. 'I was just playing around.'

'Come on, we've taken too much time, so let's get going.'

The lorries took off, backfiring smoke that smelt like something burning.

'I hope we've not been set up to ride these things that are about to self-combust and explode?' said Amy.

'I'm sure the smell is only temporary,' said Pat. 'It's probably the first time these lorries have been used.'

'Thanks Pat, for getting her off the dramatic stage. I owe you one,' said Will.

The trio floated in their lavalorries toward the hot fired up planet known as Venus. From afar she looked to be cloud covered just as they had known, but through the breaks in the clouds her magnificent colours shone. The planet was backed by a night star filled sky which emphasised her ability to shine as brightly as the moon. As planet Venus neared Amy noticed movement in her peripheral vision so she turned her head for a closer inspection.

'I don't believe it. I mean I see it, but I don't believe it.'

'What are you on about Ames?'

'Look!'

'Do you mean...'

'Yes. It looks as if we're on a direct collision course with that moving object. We need to change course.'

'Don't panic, Amy. There'll be a way.'

'These things have wheels,' pointed out Will.

'Yes, we've not yet landed on Venus and we're still floating so the benefit of the wheels has not kicked in,' said Pat patiently.

The collision seemed inevitable as the object was moving faster and faster toward the three lavalorries. Pat looked at his dash and nudged his hot/cold lever ever so slightly toward the hot direction. A large black diamond appeared with words written in green letters.

"Touch Panel."

Pat placed his paw on the far right of his diamond and his lavalorry steered in that direction. He lapped back and came between Will and Amy.

'Move the hot/cold lever slightly off cold.'

'What?' screamed Amy.

'I said...' Pat had moved too far into the atmosphere.

'What did he say Will?'

'Move the hot/cold handle to just above completely cold.'

'Then what?'

Will had moved on as Amy looked down and saw the black diamond had appeared. She didn't see the instructions as her eyes darted back to the object that was just metres away. Clumsily she slammed her hand down on the dash which glided her lorry out of harm's way and back beside Will.

'Watch out Amy; it's heading back for us. That thing's travelling so fast it's a blur when it passes, so I can't make out what it is.'

The object came back, skidding closely between Will and Amy's lorries then doubling back to pass by Pat's, sending all three into a stationary twirl. Once the spinning ceased, Will frantically placed his hands on the black diamond control panel, trying to figure how to increase his speed.

'If they can move at that pace then so can we.'

Another press on the panel shot the answer up on the screen and Will was away. Speed had never bothered him; the faster the better. Amy and Pat both witnessed Will's action so they did the same.

Will tailgated the fast-moving object, then he heard the engine kick in. He was determined to catch up so increased his speed to maximum which temporarily blurred his vision. This made it impossible to work out who or what they were following.

The chase continued, then the front object swerved, taking a severe 360 degree turn direct at Will. Within centimetres a voice screamed.

'Stop please stop, I'm going to be sick.'

Phew! Will thought, as he feared for his life.

The object darted off then turned around and came back at a sensible speed, angling up beside Will's lorry.

'Ha! You thought I was going to hit you.'

Will waited for his eyes to refocus, then said, 'Hugh is that you?'

'Who else would it be?'

'Hi Will.'

'And Reece?'

'Yep we're both here.'

'Why the hell did you scare me like that, Hugh? I thought I was gone.'

'Well, lots of things have changed since you came to Mercury. I've learnt how to push these anyshapecarts to excessive speeds, and it brings out the thrill seeker in me.'

Reece rolled her eyes. 'Yes, and outrageous fear in me. I have to shut my eyes and hope for the best every time he's in control.'

'I bet you do Reece. It's so good to see you, but what are you doing here?'

Amy and Pat headed over, just in time to hear Reece say, 'We got word you were coming back and since we wanted to see you again, here we are.'

Hugh's eyes lit up at the sight of Amy. 'Hi Amy,' he said.

Amy smiled.

'Come on tronbeings,' said Will. 'Explain. How did you hear of our return?'

'Paatron found out and told us.'

'Wait... he found out and then let you come here?'

'Yep.'

'Is that the same Ry we met that wouldn't let you out of his sight let alone out of Zola and now you're free to roam around the universe on your own?'

'Yep Will, same one.'

'I don't believe it Reece, what happened?'

'After you left, Hugh grew up,' said Reece as she darted her gaze toward Hugh and back.

Hugh slumped in his seat.

'We all went to work. Lev, Uma, Jem and I went with Maatron to the rock village while Paatron, Hugh and Jock worked in the iron village. Even though I don't like to admit it Hugh worked the longest and the hardest.'

'I always had it in me,' put in High. 'I didn't want to be taken advantage of.'

'As if, Hugh,' commented Will.

Amy rolled her eyes. 'What happened then Reece?'

'You'd be proud. We've built so many new buildings and the tronmunity is getting along really well.'

'That all sounds wonderful, but back to the original question, what are you doing here? I thought anyshapecarts were exclusive only to Mercury?'

Hugh decided to tell the rest of the story. 'Paatron told us you were coming. How he found out we don't know. It took a lot of convincing but we got permission from Mercury to allow us to take this anyshapecart off the planet.'

'Hey, I've ridden in those anyshapecarts and they never went as fast as you two were going.'

'Making these things move has been my speciality. I have worked and developed the technology to get these things up to speed. Unctrons Stan, Fell, Ash and Linx have all contributed and have been a fount of knowledge but it was me who worked out the final solution.'

'Is that true Reece?' asked Amy.

'I know it's hard to believe, but it's true.'

Hugh expressed a proud look directly at Amy.

'I got to hand it to you Hugh. The last time we met you were a spoilt brat.'

'I was Will and I'm ashamed of myself for that. I can't change what I was in the past but I want to help you.'

'In what way?' questioned Will suspiciously. 'Hugh, what do you know?'

'Nothing.'

'Really?'

'Honestly Will. I've not heard anything more than you guys were going to be here. I'm pretty sure that's all Paa and Maatron knew.'

'Ah kids, all four of you... I think we should get going. I heard an angry roar,' said Pat.

'I didn't hear a thing.'

'Don't worry Reece, you'll get used to Pat's supersonic hearing. He can hear and see things that no one else can.'

'Oh okay then. Where to?'

'To Venus,' replied Amy, 'isn't it obvious?'

'Cool! Venus,' said Hugh excitedly. 'I've not been to any of the other planets before.'

'Can we really go with you?' asked Reece.

'Not sure I guess we'll find out. Come as far as you can with us and if you get turned away then so be it.'

Hugh and Reece were rapt with excitement as Hugh glanced at their anyshapecart.

'The only condition we have use of this anyshapecart is that it's not to go onto the surface of any other planet. It can remain in the atmosphere or on Mercury but that's it.'

'Why, does your registration run out if you land on another planet?'

'Actually Will, it does. Mercury knows we are here and as long as the anyshapecart stays in the territory it should, he'll be cool. Cyril on the other hand doesn't know we're here. I'm not sure what his policy is on tronbeings visiting another planet.'

The word TILOAPS thumped into Will's head.

'I guess it's up to you, Hugh. Are you coming with us, or waiting for Cyril's approval?'

'We're with you Will.'

'That sound's getting louder so we need to move,' put in Pat.

Amy scratched and fidgeted with her headband because it was annoying her. 'Hugh, you travel with Will and Reece you come with me.'

Hugh flung her a look of sheer disappointment but Amy ignored him and moved on.

Will manoeuvred his lorry over so Hugh could climb in then Amy came up on the other side, providing an easy transition for Reece.

'I'm so happy to hang out with you again. I've really missed you,' said Reece.

'But now that you live on the surface haven't you made lots of friendtrons?'

'I have but you were my first one ever.'

'Let me guess; you never forget your first friendtron right?'

'Right.'

'They say it's like you never forget your first kiss.'

'I guess so Amy. I've not reached that stage.'

'Me either. You know, Will often talks about his best buddy when he was younger. He was called Zac. They don't see one another anymore, but Will says Zac is the reason for his space obsession.'

'What else has he said about him?'

'This part is spooky. They made this pact when they were younger that Will thinks about all the time, I know he does cause I can see it in his eyes. He's told me the word that describes the pact. It's something like TILPA or TOLPA, but you'd have to ask Will the exact word.'

'What does it mean?'

'Cyril says the pact is to prove and/or preserve the TILAP word. Will won't tell us what it means and now he is compelled to keep it a secret. Cyril says if he reveals to anyone what it is before he proves it or preserves it or both harm will come to all three of us.'

'Why would anyone want to harm the magic trio?'

Amy smiled at Reece's description of herself, Pat and Will. 'Don't know all the reasons but mainly it's got to do with the magnifier. The good news for you, Reece, is that you're able to get out and stay safe.'

'No way; you helped us when we needed it so now we're here to help you.'

'Do you really know what you're going into? You may not return to Ry and Jean and the life you have just learned about and love living.'

'I don't care. You don't know either.'

Amy shot an astonished look at Reece then took a huge gulp into the back of her throat as thoughts whirled through her mind. 'Reece, I guess what doesn't kill you makes you stronger, right?'

'Right.'

Amy removed her headband and rubbed her head. 'That's better. It's annoying me today for some reason.'

'I'll wear it for a while, if it's okay with you,' said Reece. 'I've always thought your headband was cool.'

'Okay,' agreed Amy as they shared a giggle.

'I'm so excited. What are we going to do on Venus?'

'I guess since you've decided to join us I should let you know about our mission. As you remember, we got one when we visited Mercury and now Cyril has given us one for Venus.' Amy went through the first seven letters of the alphabet remembering each one and the task assigned to that letter.

'Wow, sounds like we'll be a long time on Venus,' commented Reece.

'That part really worried me when we on Mercury but time stands still on Earth while we're here. I don't know how it works on Mercury.'

'Probably not the same but Paa and Maatron know where we are.'

That's better than for Will and me, Amy thought.

'So Will what are these things called?' asked Hugh.

'Good old Cyril told us they're lavalorries.'

'Don't know how good he is but he sure is old. Anyway great name, lavalorries.' Hugh smiled. 'Remember; I've learnt how to make the anyshapecarts go faster. I love knowing how things move.'

'You're like a mechanic.'

'Kind of I guess. I like both the mechanical and the electronic side.'

'Things must have really changed on Mercury. You barely had electricity when we were there.'

'We have more than we used to,' Hugh drew a quick breath. 'I invented ways to make the carts move faster using small portions... until the supply to our planet becomes larger.'

Will noticed Hugh was puffing. 'What's up with your breathing?'

'This smoke is hard to breathe. Mercury is a notoriously hot planet but the heat here is stifling.'

'Firstly it's not smoke; it's steam and secondly, hold on.'

Will went to his control panel and shot his lavalorry directly upwards. 'The steam on the upper level will stop your breathlessness and return your energy to you. I'm taking you there now.'

Smart thinking and a swift move on Will's part saw Hugh's breathing return to normal.

'It's just something I learnt on the way,' Will explained. 'Also, Cyril told us what our mission is.'

'You have a mission?'

'Sure, what do you think we're sent here for? A good time?'

'Absolutely Will. That's exactly what I thought.'

'We do have a great time but I'll explain the mission.' Will relayed all the details to Hugh. 'Now let's try and catch up to the others.'

As the lorries neared each other a shaft of bright light hit Amy's crystal ring, causing it to fly open. A large message displayed in the sky.

'NEARING VENUS.'

'OMG Amy is that normal?' asked Reece. 'I mean that ring. Is it normal on Earth for a ring to give a message like the one we just saw?'

'No, but up here strange things like that happen all the time. You'll get used to it. That headband you're wearing has some of the same features.'

Will edged his lorry in line with Amy's.

'Why did you two shoot upwards before?'

'Hugh found it hard to breathe.'

Amy couldn't miss this opportunity. 'Hugh, don't steal my limelight. It's normally me that struggles to breathe.'

'Guess it was my turn this time round.'

'Follow me,' screamed Pat who was just out in front.

The cloud cover was intense and fortunately Pat knew to stay high until he found a comfortable breathing level. The others followed.

CHAPTER FOUR
VENNIS

The three lavalorries came out of the thick steam and hit the surface of Venus with a jolt causing Hugh and Reece to be tossed to the base of what looked to be a very large volcano. Will, Pat and Amy pulled up close by and ran to assist.

'Are you okay, Reece?'

'I'm fine. I'm made of rock you know so I have a tendency to crumble but that wasn't a hard enough landing.'

Amy laughed as they both hopped back into their lorry.

'Hugh buddy, are you okay?'

Hugh rolled over so he was face down and remained there for a while.

'Hugh, what's going on?' questioned Will.

'This small hole in the ground is letting out steam. Give me a second, I'm starting to feel better.'

'Are you hurt?'

Hugh slightly lifted his head. 'I'm made of iron. I've got more chance of melting, but a few scratches ain't going to make any difference.'

'OMG!'

'What's up Will?'

'I remember being taught that the surface of Venus is so hot, it can melt a solid block of lead or iron. Get up Hugh, get up.' Will yanked him to his feet.

'Okay but right now I feel fine. That steam pod really helped.'

Pat noticed a yellow rock had popped out of the surface right beside Hugh's left foot. 'Watch out for that rock,' he warned.

It was too late. Hugh had unintentionally dragged his foot over the rock and seated himself in the lorry. A large white net came out of the ground, capturing the three lorries and escalating them upwards.

Will peered down. 'The net's on a giant pole. That is what's pushing us upwards.'

The team looked down until they felt themselves stop, positioned beside the top of the volcano.

'I've never seen the inside of a volcano before,' said Amy.

'Let's hope it's not active, otherwise we're history.'

'It doesn't look to be active Pat.'

Around the net a giant oval frame appeared. It formed on both sides at the same time and met at the top. Next the net tightened to the frame but left enough tension to hold the lorries.

'We've been caught in a volcano-sized tennis racquet. Look down; the base is the same as a handle, then there's the long shaft and the net part,' said Will.

'The strings on a tennis racquet are normally much tighter than these.'

'True Ames, but if they were any tighter our lavalorries wouldn't hold.'

Hugh and Reece didn't know what tennis was so they just listened while Pat looked down to where they had come from and noticed rubbish and rocks dumped. It looked like a wasteland.

Will noticed a stack of grey lava rocks that looked to be the same shape. They were hidden behind the volcano they were looking into. One of the rocks was facing upwards on the pile and he noted a part of an image had been etched into it. He was about to point it out to the others when Pat spoke.

'I wonder what we're supposed to do now.'

'That's the million dollar question Pat; surely someone will let us know something and with luck we won't be stuck up here for too long.'

'What's your hurry, Will? Have you some place you need to be?'

'Not at all Pat, but it is hot.'

'Good, then take it in and enjoy it.'

'It's hard to see through the cloud cover.'

'I beg to differ Will; I think if we hang here a bit we might get some ABCDEF clues.'

'There's the reason it's so good having you here, Pat,' said Amy. 'You're always on the job.'

'Thanks Amy. I need you all to be aware that we have been lifted up here for a reason. In life there are no free rides.'

'Getting up here was a free ride.'

'I promise it wasn't; always remember there are no free rides.'

Between the shaft and the racquet there was a ledge where an unusual being sat.

'Look down there. What is that?' puzzled Will.

'I'm guessing it's one of the aliens that live on this planet,' answered Pat.

'Seeing that alien makes me understand how weird it must have been for you three when you first met me,' said Hugh.

'It's still weird,' joked Amy.

'It looks as though he's talking on a two way radio. Tune your ears in Pat. What's he saying?'

'I can go one better Will. Watch this.'

Pat pressed a few buttons on the black diamond on his lavalorry, noticed a speaker on the dash and was able to tune into the frequency.

'Are our lavalorries fitted with two way radios?' asked Will as he searched around on his dash, engaging the black diamond for instructions. 'Here, I found it. Come in Amy. Over.'

'Will, I'm right here in the lorry beside you.'

'I know, but let's give the two way a go so if we're separated, we can communicate.'

'Great theory, but it will only work within a certain range.'

The team tested the two way ensuring it worked on each of the lorries, and in their investigations they also found they had the function of a built in camera.

A conversation came through.

'This is a record Max, we've got three. Finally a proper game of vennis. How long until you're ready? Over.'

'Not long Jack, I'm just getting across to my vacket now. Over.'

'The cloud cover is so thick, we won't see our shots once we've hit them. Over.'

'And that's why we had to con Tom into doing our commentating. He'll amuse himself and keep us up to date on the score. Speaking of which I wonder where he is. Over.'

'Hey Max, which vacket did you decided to use? Over.'

'I went with your suggestion. I'm using the one between your famnic's twin Slava Slopes. It was already up so there was no need to erect it. Over.'

'But how did you get up to it? Over.'

'I hitched a ride up on Slava Slope one. The Mosaic Moveator was working so I jumped on it, then walked across the small bridge between slope one and two. You know what I'm talking about, it's the same bridge we've had spitting competitions from. Over.'

'Please tell me you got up without Maanic seeing you. Over.'

'Chill will you. Your maanic was way too busy. Over.'

Jack sighed into the two way. Will and Amy, the tronbeings and Pat weren't sure what to make of what they'd just heard.

'I wonder what vennis and a vacket are. I've never heard of them before. Then again living on Mercury there's lots of things I've never heard of.'

'Don't be hard on yourself Reece, there's plenty of things I've never heard of either, I don't know what vennis...' Amy went silent for a moment. 'I've got it.' Everyone looked at her as she once again checked out the large oval frame and the net they were caught it.

'What is it Ames?'

'Tennis. They're going to play their version of a game of tennis, except they're calling it vennis which my guess is either V for volcano or V for Venus.'

'Well done Amy. I think you've guessed that right, but hang on, I think they're intending to use us as the ball or do they call them valls?' asked Pat.

'What?' questioned Hugh.

'On Earth we have a game called tennis. It's played on a proper court which is an area where lines are painted on the ground. There are two players, one on each end and a net that spans across the middle. The players have to hit the ball over the net.'

'What do they use to hit the ball?'

'A racquet, which is a much smaller version of this that's been referred to as a vacket. Now back to my concern. I think they're intending to use us as the ball or should I say vall?'

Will shrugged. 'Pat, there's not much we can do about it from up here. Listen up everyone. Jack and Max are back on.'

'Can you see the Lava Hi House, or the twin Hotspots from where you are?'

'Hotspots yes, Hi House no. What about you Max? Over.'

'I can only see the outline of the Hi House.'

There was a pause of silence then Max continued.

'Jack, it's taken me a while but you always bags the Wasteland vacket first, how come? Over.'

'We've been friendnics for so long I can't believe you have to ask. My maanic Molly is more nosy than your paanic and maanic. They don't ask questions when you go missing during a break from mining at the Hot Spot but if Molly sees me leave the twin Slava Slopes for a second, she gives me the third degree with questions. Over.'

'Jack, that's the price we both pay while ever we work for a famnic business. Over.'

'Anyway Max, no nicbeings ever come near the wasteland and horrid Henry and his Hi House are far enough away. That's why I choose this vacket. Over.'

'This conversation between Jack and Max is really interesting,' said Pat. 'We have quite a bit of information.'

'So far they've told us they're about to play vennis and they're waiting for Tom to commentate and score for them.'

'What else, Will?'

'Jack works at the twin Slava Slopes and Max mines at the twin Hot Spots.'

'You listened properly Will.'

'Maybe, but I can't work out what they're called or the language they're using.'

'I'm sure we'll work it out.'

They fell silent again, listening.

'Tom, are you there? Over.'

'Yes Jack, it took me a while to get here, because there's a lavalorry jam near the Date Wall. One side of the land that holds the Date Wall up seems to be sinking, caving to the pressure of boiling lava. Some of the lavalorries that drove too close to the edge have fallen in. Over.'

'The Date Wall!' exclaimed Amy. 'Cyril told us clues were magnified at the Date Wall.'

'Shush up Amy, I can't hear.'

Amy poked her tongue out at Will to retaliate.

'Were any nicbeings hurt Tom? Over.'

'Jack, it would be safe to say that no nicbeing would make it out of boiling lava alive.'

'That is sad,' interrupted Max, 'but it's not our problem. We've a small window to get some vennis in so now you can commentate, Tom, and keep the score while I beat Jack.'

'Ha ha Max, we'll see about that,' added Jack.

The conversation between Jack, Max and Tom ceased as Will turned to Pat.

'We know they mine for something at the twin Hot Spot but I wonder what the twin Slava Slopes and Mosaic Moveator are?' asked Will.

'I'd like to know who horrid Henry is,' said Amy.

'With luck, kids, we'll find out both.'

'Look at what Jack is doing down there,' said Amy. 'He's got some kind of a joy stick in his hand and he's directing it to move this vacket we're entangled in.'

The vacket moved in the same direction Jack moved his joystick.

'This is mild. I thought being a vall in a vennis match would be far more rigorous.'

'Don't speak too soon Amy, he looks to be sending an elevated platform up toward us,' said Will.

An elevated platform appeared and each of the lavalorries was gently coaxed onto it. The part of the platform that Amy's and Will's lavalorries were on was moved downwards but Pat's remained where it was.

'All right all you aquanics and libnics out there, *not that any of you are listening,* you're wound up in the Venus war that's currently taking place, and it's time for the vennis play off between friendnics Jack and Max. *Yeah the nicbeings went wild, well I'm sure they would have if only there was someone listening.*'

'Nicbeings, that's the name for the beings that live here.'

'How did you work that out Will?'

'Tom mentioned aquanics, libnics, friendnics and nicbeings. I'm guessing the aquanics are the males, the libnics are the females, nicbeings are the community as a whole and friendnics has to be friends. Zena the zodiac must have left two of her children on Venus as she did on Mercury. Here she left Aquarius and Libra.'

Amy nodded agreeing with Will's summary as Tom's commentary continued.

'So let's recap the rules, oh that's right there aren't any.'

A loud fart permeated through the speaker. 'Sorry, that was me, I couldn't hold it in. There must have been some wind in the steam!'

Hugh was in hysterics. 'Tom is so funny, he thinks he's not being heard, so he's amusing himself.'

'Our aquanics get three shots each. The aim of the game is to keep the lavalorry in play, without missing a shot. The best of three wins. They have each won one game so the winner here will be the champion. Aquanics and libnics, before play gets underway, are there any words of wisdom for our aquanics? Of course not and there's no surprises there '

'It's Jack's serve, and he's chosen the single lavalorry for his first shot '

'Will, is Pat going to be okay?'

'I hope so. We'll have to watch and see.'

'I'll quickly scan the area where all the adoring nicbeings are and yep, not a single one in sight. Okay, we're away. Jack has surged his vall through the thick cloud cover and it's directly on course between the twin Slava Slopes to Max's vacket. Max returned the serve causing Jack to move his vacket to the right. From afar it looks like that fluffy creature in the small lavalorry is digging this rally.'

Pat relished being flung from one side to the other; he was enjoying the sights of Venus when the cloud cover dispersed.

'Jack just won his first serve, *yeah the crowd cheered, at least we wished they would.*

'Anyway nicbeings moving right along Max will now store the lavalorry for one for when it's his turn to serve.'

'That's good. At least we know where Pat is,' commented Amy.

'Next vall, the lavalorry on steroids,' announced
Tom as Will's lavalorry with him and Hugh in it was
escalated up on their platform ready for the serve.

'It's time for Jack's second serve, yeah the nicbeings
are out of control, well I'm sure they would be if any
were here.'

'He is so funny Amy,' said Reece.

'I can't stop laughing at him,' agreed Amy.

'This lavalorry is so big it's straining the vackets but
Max has managed to once again return Jack's hit this
time a little off course. Goodness nicbeings, these
friendnics are both playing to win. And it's a hit back
then back again and yes Jack takes out his second shot.
The score is 2-0 in favour of Jack. If you can't hear the
nicbeings cheering, don't check your hearing aid.'

'Wow Amy, it's our turn and I'm nervous.'

'Don't worry too much. The others looked to be
okay.' Amy looked at her headband on Reece's head.
'Actually Reece can I have my headband back? I want to
stop my hair from flying into my eyes.'

'Sure Amy, here you go.'

'Shot three is up for Jack, the sleek sports lavalorry.
What a contradiction that is. Anyway moving right along
Jack has flung it out of sight, well not really, as it's on its
way back. This rally is heating up!'

'Being the vall was great, Hugh; did you enjoy it?'

'Absolutely amazing fun.'

'Yeah, Jack won three out of three a perfect score.
That's awesometacular. Now it's up to Max. The
pressure is on as he serves up the sports lorry just
clearing the twin Slava Slopes. Phew, that was close.
Jack returns it then Max hits back. Well done Max; one
out of one. Next he serves up the single lorry and wait…
he aces it on his first shot. The atmosphere here is

electrifying, well it would be if I had some nicbeings to share it with.

'Okay Max; this is your last vall, the oversized lavalorry and it's off but wait... a burning lava rock has collided into it. Knocking it off course but it adjusted and went straight into Jack's vacket where it was returned. Not sure what's happening. Henry must have it in for this lavalorry as he's aimed and hit it again, this time it has bounced off the top of the Date Wall which would not be good for the sinking land underneath it and went straight into Max's vacket. Oh I can see nicbeings near to the Date Wall have just seen that bounce. This is turning into a remarkable game of vennis. I've not seen anything like it. Max takes the shot and soars the lavalorry back to Jack who can't return the serve. That's it, we have a tie, and what a sensational game it was especially that last rally. Guess I'll be back next time when Jack and Max scam me into commentating to no nicbeings. Bye for now.'

After the match was over, Jack put all three lavalorries in line with his vacket and flung them off.

'Where did you fling them to, Jack? Over.'

'I looked at the Lava Hi House. The cloud had lifted a little and I noticed one of the garage doors was open so I flung them there.'

'Jack, that's into the hands of the enemy. You know how grumpy and nasty Henry is.'

'So? We don't even know who or what they are so who cares what happens to them?'

'Hey friendnics, sorry to interrupt this enthralling conversation but I've got to go. That grumpy so and so you've just spoken about is my boss and he lets me and my paanic get away with nothing, even though Paanic has worked for him forever.'

'Tom, just before you go, was he kind to you when your maanic died?'

'Not at all Jack, he's as greedy as ever and he'll never change. Why do you think there is so much fighting on Venus?'

'Thanks for the game aquanics. See you soon.'

'Bye Tom. I've got to go too. See you later, Jack.'

'Bye Max.'

CHAPTER FIVE
LAVA HI HOUSE

The three lavalorries swooped into a wide opening that looked like a garage. Once inside, the door slammed shut. They stood in complete darkness except for Pat's collar that was glowing.

'That vennis was unbelievable. I never realised being the vall could be so much fun.'

'Come on Reece, Tom made it with his humour,' added Hugh.

'My favourite part was the sight of Venus when there was a break in the cloud cover,' commented Pat.

'It was awesometacular.'

'Is that your new favourite buzz word Ames?'

'Sure is, Will.'

Pat thought Will sounded a bit dejected. 'What's up, Will? Didn't you enjoy the vennis?'

'It was remarkable Pat, but I'd like to know who threw the burning lava rocks that hit my lorry, because bouncing off the Date Wall was not that much fun.'

'That would be me. How did you all get in here?' asked a stern cross voice.

'Where are we?' asked Pat but there was no answer.

All five climbed out of their lavalorries and followed the voice. The door out came up to Amy's waist and Will's hip so they bent themselves in half and crawled through. Once inside there was a never ending spiral staircase that went up through the middle of the very tall extremely narrow circular building. Evenly spaced around the outside of the landing they were standing on were five doors, all the same colour and size as the one they had come through.

Each door had large capital letters on it. They had come through the one with N/LHH. The other doors had E/THS, S/TSS, W/W and C/DW. The building was constructed from dark grey lava cobblestones as was the spiral staircase.

The stern voice had remained behind in the dark room they had come from so Pat whispered to the others, 'I'm guessing the first of those letters on the doors stand for North, East, South and West but I can't work out what C is for.'

They nodded to agree.

Will was deep in thought. 'Could C be for centre? I'm just guessing here, Pat.'

Pat thought some more until he came forth with the answer. 'I think you're right Will. Here's how it works; N/LHH stands North Lava Hi House, E/THS is East Twin Hot Spots, S/TSS is South Twin Slava Slopes W/W is West Wasteland and C/DW is Centre Date Wall.'

'That makes sense, Pat, but I wonder why there is a huge red cross that looks like spray paint over the C/DW door?'

'I don't know, Will.'

They all hushed as a tall, large, very unattractive and dishevelled aquanic entered the room and paced about. He was an older vintage and his body was made of light grey lava. His distinguishing feature was a small circular window on his chest that was half filled with blue steam. It looked like a porthole and on the top middle of his back as he half turned there was a spout. This was the first time they had been close enough to see the characteristics of a nicbeing so they all stared.

'Y'all, how did you get into my Hi House?'

Reece and Amy laughed, as they'd never heard such an accent.

'What's so funny?' he demanded and that shut the laughter off.

Pat realised he was grumpy but was relieved that he knew where they were.

'I just asked how you got in here; no nicbeing ever gets in here,' he screamed at them.

They were all petrified, including Pat, but he knew he had to say something. 'We were flung here by accident from the vennis vacket,' he said.

'Who flung you?' This time he didn't scream the question.

'Ahh we don't know, we were just flung,' said Will.

'The only reason you got in is because the other one like you,' he said as he pointed his chin toward Will, 'left the garage door open, the silly idiot.'

Will's ears pricked up. 'Another one like me; what does that mean?'

'It means the other one like you.'

'Henry, what's going on up there?'

Amy and Reece were closest to an open trapdoor in the floor where this voice came from so they looked down.

If you've seen him you should see her...she's not much better, Amy thought.

'We've got unwelcome things here Hillary. You just mind your own business.'

'I will not mind my own business, Henry, when you're screeching at the top of your voice.'

'What do you want?'

'I want to know who you're talking to, as we both know you are devoid of any social skills.'

'Mind your own business. What do you want anyway?'

'I need help lifting these ven-la-rocs.'

Amy saw she was buckling under the weight of them.

'Also, the volcano is indicating an oversupply of static electricity. It's not called *the Indicator* for nothing.'

'Good. Keep your mouth shut Hillary, until I get these pests out of here.'

'I'd be happy to give Hillary a hand lifting. It would save you the trouble,' said Amy.

'Go on then.'

Will looked directly at Amy who returned the stare. They were such good friends they could speak to each other without even talking. Reece, not to be left behind, followed Amy without a murmur as Henry watched in disagreeable silence.

Pat worked out Henry was greedy and selfish and that he controlled Venus's electricity. They were obviously there on borrowed time but Pat was determined to push for answers.

'Henry, why is there a big red cross on the C/DW door?'

'One almost down thanks to that oversized lavalorry and two to go. Soon those stupid nicbeings will stop protesting and pelting lava bullets and shovels at my Hi House. They'll have to work for me, as they'll have no other options once I've destroyed their existence. Things will be done my way without change.'

'What are you going to do?' asked Will, swallowing his distaste at this unpleasant being.

'It's not what I'm going to do. It's what I've already done.'

'How many nicbeings work for you Henry?'

'Most of the planet but I want full control. I already control the electricity supply and the ven-la-rocs. I just need control of the twin Slava Slopes that produce the running lava and the Hot Spot that mines for precious gems. Once they're mine, everything will be done the way I want it done and if the nicbeings don't like it they'll be banished to the Wasteland.'

Pat had never come in contact with a character like Henry. He was a real control freak. 'Henry, you mentioned the other one like him,' he said as he pointed at Will. 'Where is he?'

'He works for me now—came here looking for work so I gave it to him.'

'What sort of work?' asked Hugh.

'The kind you don't need to know about.'

Will was nervous. The longer they stayed the more risk there seemed of getting caught here. He looked to Pat who appeared cool and calm and was about to launch into another question.

'Where do you want me to put these, Hillary?' asked Amy politely. 'They're heavy.'

'Stop complaining. You offered to help. Put them here.'

As Amy placed her overflowing tray of ven-la-rocs on the bench Hillary had allocated, a couple fell to the floor. Reece put her tray beside Amy's and noticed Amy had quickly picked some fallen ones up and shoved them into her pocket. Reece did the same while Hillary's back was turned.

'What does that scale on your back do?' Amy asked, still politely. 'I noticed Henry has a spout on his back.'

'You really are new here,' responded Hillary as she half turned from what she was doing then turned back and continued. 'All libnics are females, all aquanics are males. Whether you have a spout or a scale alludes to what you are. I am a scalelibnic and Henry is spoutaquanic. The aquanics have blue steam inside their porthole on the front chest and we have yellow steam. Our brain sends a message we are low on steam and the steam comes from boiling lava. Spoutnics can collect boiling lava by leaning their back near the flow of it down the side of the twin Slava Slopes and use it for themselves or pour the lava onto the tray of a scalenic. If scalenics need steam they can use their scale to scrape lava from the ground, then once it starts to harden we dispose of it.'

'You drop it just anywhere?' asked Amy.

'Yes, it blends with the surface. Now stop taking up my time and get over here and carry some more ven-la-rocs.'

Amy and Reece did as they were told but typically, Amy couldn't keep her mouth shut. 'I love that amethyst ring on your finger. Amethyst is my favourite stone. Where did you get it?'

Hillary put her hand up to admire it. 'Back when Henry was a much kinder aquanic, before he became so greed-hungry and selfish, he found matching stones that are faultless. They are the only two of their kind as no others as superior as these have ever been found. He gave one to me and one for my—' She quickly stopped the sentence. 'I don't know what he did with the other one.'

Amy and Reece widened their eyes as they looked at each other.

'How did you get the name nicbeings?' asked Amy.

'The last three letters from the word volcanic, idiot,' was all Hillary answered.

'What's in those boxes?'

'Do you ever stop asking questions?' Hillary looked at Amy with her hand on her hip.

'Just one more.' Amy raised her index finger. Hillary rolled her eyes. 'Those boxes over there. What are they?'

'The boxes are made of lava that comes from the twin Slava Slopes. We pack portions of static electricity and the nicbeings that work for us deliver them to the twin Hot Spots and the twin Slava Slopes.'

'But they are only portions... surely electricity needs to free flow so it can be used whenever needed.'

'You said one more question and you're slacking off on your duties; hop to work.'

'Please, just tell me why you only deliver it in portions and since there is no entrance to this Hi House how do the nicbeings get the boxes to deliver?'

'For goodness' sake! I have ways through my domain down here to get the boxes outside for the nicbeings to deliver. No nicbeings have been inside here for a very long time, which is why I was surprised when I heard Henry talking. In answer to the last part of your question, Henry doesn't want to change. This is how he's always done it. He wants to deliver portions because that way he controls how long manufacturing can be done for. I don't know why I'm telling you so much and it's none of your damn business.'

Amy ignored Hillary's last comment. She felt there was a soft side to Hillary and if she kept communicating with her maybe it would come out.

'But that's not fair,' she protested.

'It's the way it is. Now, silence and back to work.'

Amy was astounded with what she'd seen so far. She kept looking around and noticed one almighty ven-la-roc. It was ginormous and sitting in the corner of the room near where they were working. It was so big it would take two humans to lift it. Aware she had reached her question quota with Hillary, she pushed her luck.

'Hillary, is that the largest ven-la-roc in the history of Venus?'

Hillary looked to where Amy was pointing, admiring it as though it was one of her offspring. 'That's my treasure. It's a one off. How it formed I don't know. I've never got anything nearly the same size as this one ever. It's so bold and beautiful and so large, it could blast through anything.'

Amy was shocked as the word *blast* had resonated with her.

That is what the letter B stands for in our mission, she noted to herself.

With that, Amy's headband heated up and her ring went crazy, spinning around out of control.

Away in Henry's quarters, the fan on Will's wristband nearly sent his wrist into orbit, the magnifier nearly burnt a hole in his bum and Pat's collar nearly choked him as it ran rings around his neck. At the same time deafening sirens vibrated from the very top of the Hi House down the spiral staircase and through the floor. Henry bolted up the stairs as fast as his fat legs could take him.

'Amy,' Will screamed, 'are you okay?'

'Yes Will, we're fine.'

'We need to get out of here.'

'Got it Will.'

Amy and Reece saw Hillary open a secret door that looked like part of the floor. She ushered them out. On the way Amy screamed, 'Will, get Hugh to take my lorry and we'll see you out front.'

Amy and Reece crawled through a slimy narrow passageway barely wide enough for them to fit through while Will, Pat and Hugh used the magnifier to find the switch to open the garage door to free them.

As soon as they were out in the clear, Will said, 'Phew, I am so relieved to be out of there.'

Amy and Reece came to the surface through a small door about the same size as the one they had used to enter.

'Look Reece, this door has three keyholes. It takes three keys to open it. I bet we can get out but not back in through this way unless we have the keys.'

'Probably,' agreed Reece, 'and I'm sure Hillary and Henry are the only two who know where those keys are.'

They were slightly disorientated but worked out they were inside the Indicator; the volcano into which the Hi House was built. Fortunately the level they were at was only piles of rocks and no activity. They worked out how to get out of there.

'What is going on Reece? Something bad must really be happening.'

'I know. I keep getting shoved aside by the nicbeings. There are thousands of them that look as if they're going in the same direction. I wonder what happened?'

The Lava Hi House's siren was ear-splitting and nicbeings were screaming.

'No idea Reece, let's find the others.'

Amy ran in front of Reece around to the front of the Lava Hi House where they discovered Will, Pat and Hugh. Reece jumped in with Will while Amy went with Hugh.

'What's happened?' Amy called to Will.

'There's a problem at the Date Wall. Hurry, follow me.'

They took off in single file on a mission.

'Keep your eyes ahead Reece so I can see if this lavalorry comes with a built in GPS,' said Will.

'Ugh!' she responded but Will ignored her and manipulated the screen in all ways sorting through the options.

Pat had the same thought pattern except his collar assisted.

'Head to the west where the surface is smoother.'

Pat's collar had kicked in with instructions so he held down the button on his two way. 'Come in Will and Amy.'

'What's up? Over,' replied Will.

'My collar's giving the instructions, so follow me. Amy do you read?'

'Got it Pat, over.'

Pat's lorry bounced along. It was so light the surface was not a problem for him. Will's lorry was so large it rode over everything. Amy and Hugh struggled and were slipping further behind as the sports version was too low to the ground so every hump and bump was felt. Loose rocks from the surface kept skimming up underneath and the dust from the flurry hindered their vision.

'We're losing speed Amy; the others are so much further ahead.'

Amy dived for the two way button. 'Will and Pat can you hear me?' There was no response so she panicked and tried again. 'Will and Pat please do you read me?'

She saw them as faint shadows in the distance and received no response.

Then the lorry they were in stopped and tears filled Amy's eyes. 'We've broken down and Will and Pat can't hear me,' she told Hugh.

Hugh jumped out and crawled underneath to try to work out where the problem was while Amy hopped out as well and took a short wander with her arms crossed and her head down, noticing how deserted the area was.

She felt something underneath her foot so bent down, brushed some of the rock chips away and picked it up. It took her seconds to recognise that it was the third key that unlocked the statues on Mercury, the one she had lost.

How did that get here?

She looked around for Hugh but he was still under the lorry so she put the key into a secret compartment she had on her along with the other two, noting to herself to tell Will and Pat as soon as she was with them again.

Hugh struggled with a large rock that was jammed in an inopportune spot that blocked the major workings of the lorry. He wedged it back and forth until he freed it and then came up with it in his hand.

'Amy I've found the culprit. Amy, Amy, Amy where are you?' He looked around but she was nowhere in sight. He checked underneath the lorry. 'Amy, Amy,' he screamed but no response.

Where is she? Hugh panicked, and dashed off in the direction he thought Amy had gone, following scuff marks where pebbles had been kicked aside. A sparkle from the surface caught his eye so he bent down and picked up her purple ring. He'd often noticed her looking through it and admiring it so surely she wouldn't just drop it?

Now he was more nervous than ever. Something must have happened to her. He had to catch the others but he knew this lorry was too slow. A wave of inspiration came over him as he lowered himself underneath and clicked a lever that was a familiar feature also on the anyshapecarts, then he made a few other small adjustments to enhance the speed. He took off.

CHAPTER SIX
THE DATE WALL
GETS SUCKED IN

When they arrived at the Date Wall there were
thousands of nicbeings surrounding it on both sides.
Hugh scanned the crowd for Will, Pat and Reece and
was able to see them standing on the top of Will's
lavalorry. He parked his lavalorry way back and pushed
through. Meanwhile Will, Pat and Reece stared at the
large crack down the middle of the Date Wall. They
noticed the shape of a large round sinkhole that had
formed in the land around it. Centimetre by centimetre
the Date Wall sank into the hole. Each time it sank a
little more the spectators screamed.

'What's happened?' asked Will.

'It's a sinkhole,' said Pat. 'Do you know what that
is?'

'Is it when a cavity is formed by running water in the
land causing the land to cave and the structure upon it
to sink?'

'Precisely, but in this case it looks as though boiling
lava is causing the sinkhole. That large crack down the
middle wouldn't help. Now the structure is divided it
will probably sink quicker.'

'Poor nicbeings; the Date Wall seems to be pretty
major for them.' Will turned to see Hugh scrambling up
the side of the lavalorry. 'Where's Amy?'

'She's gone. I think she was taken.'

'What do you mean? She was with you.'

'We broke down. I crawled underneath to work out what was wrong and when I got up Amy was gone. I didn't hear any other voices and I didn't see any lavalorries come past.'

'Far out Hugh! You're an idiot. How could you lose her like that?'

'I swear that's what happened.'

'So you're saying she just disappeared into thin air.'

'Pretty much.'

Will was furious. 'Hugh you're a useless lying, cheating—'

'Hold up Will. Look at him; he's as worried as you.'

'Do you really think I would let anything happen to Amy on purpose?'

'He's got a point Will,' interjected Pat.

'What are we going to do?' asked Hugh.

'Find her of course.'

Will sat down into the seat of his lavalorry as Reece clamped her hands to her face and Hugh stood there feeling useless because Amy went missing on his watch.

Pat was determined to try and piece everything together. 'Okay, we all need to take stock and gather facts.'

'Right,' agreed Hugh, 'has anyone got anything?'

Will had his hand on his forehead and he felt the magnifier stick into him so put the other hand on his pocket while he recited Cyril's final words. *Magnified at the date wall.'*

Will jumped to his feet and pushed his arm out in front of him. Pat watched on.

'We're at the Date Wall and it's going down. Clues are magnified here.'

Pat shrugged. 'Not sure that is going to help you now.'

'There sinks that clue!' Will really looked dejected. 'I don't get why they or she or he or whoever took Amy. Why Amy? She didn't hurt anyone. What happens if I can't find her or worse still she gets hurt?'

'Standing around worrying is not going to help,' said Pat. 'We need to do something, but right now it's pretty crowded and the Date Wall is sinking further and further.'

Will jumped out of his lorry. He stomped around until he literally bumped into an aquanic who stood staring at him.

'What are you staring at? Haven't you seen a human before?'

'No, I haven't,' the aquanic replied. He didn't like the tone of Will's voice so decided to continue staring at him and did not move out of his way.

'What do you want; the award for being able to stare the longest?'

The aquanic put his hand out. 'Calm down buddy, can't you see I've got enough angst to deal with here? I don't know what's with you but the one monument you're in charge of hasn't just been destroyed.'

Will scowled. 'You're in charge of the Date Wall?'

'Yep, I'm Marky,' he said as he still held out his hand, then added, 'and you're the one that caused the crack and in turn the accelerated slide of my Date Wall.'

'What? Me?' Will shook Marky's hand. 'Anyway, I'm Will.'

Pat, Reece and Hugh looked down to where Will was and saw him talking to a nicbeing. They quickly climbed down to be by his side to ensure he didn't say anything he'd regret.

'What are you talking about Marky? I didn't cause that crack.'

'Yeah you did. That's your lavalorry right?' Marky pointed to Will's giant lavalorry.

'I was standing here when you and your lorry came flying over and bounced off the middle of my already weakened Date Wall and produced that enormous big crack down the middle.' He glared at Will. 'What do you think the effect of 10 tonnes of lava is when it hits solid rock at reckless speeds?'

Will replied, 'I guess it cracks.'

'It wasn't his fault. He was swooped up into a game of vennis. He didn't volunteer to be the vall,' put in Pat in Will's defence.

'That is one thing I do know and I also saw the burning lava rocks that were hurled at you. Still, you should probably lie low as there's many nicbeings that will be blaming you.'

'Wait up, you said your name was Marky, right?'

'That's right.'

'I'm Pat, this is Hugh, Reece and you've already met Will.'

They all nodded, acknowledging the introduction.

'We don't know a lot about the Date Wall so can you tell us about it?'

'Sure, since it's currently sinking and there's not a thing I can do to save it. Venus used to be a land with oceans. That was until they all dried up. Since we no longer had water we learnt to survive on the steam from boiling lava but to mark the time it happened the Date Wall was erected. An image of a spoutaquanic with the spout on his back filled with water was etched into one side and an image of a scalelibnic with a pail full of water on her scale was etched on the other side.'

'What are those spouts and scales on your backs used for?' asked Hugh.

'I know,' volunteered Reece as she quickly explained to the others about how the steam worked,
what the spouts and scales were and how they worked. She explained the portholes, why nicbeings were called nicbeings and anything else she could think of that she and Amy had discussed with Hillary.

Marky listened intently, amazed by her wealth of knowledge. 'How did you learn all of that?'

'Hillary from the Lava Hi House told me.'

Marky's face went into shock. 'How did you get near her? Her husband Henry is the most despised aquanic on Venus. We can't stand him, and no nicbeing has set foot into the Hi House in a very long time.'

'How about Hillary?' questioned Reece.

'She's not as bad as him. They weren't always bad, anyway. When they were younger they were the friendliest down to Venus nicbeings. They attended vennis matches, supported nicbeings and helped out where they could. That volcano the Lava Hi House is built into is known as the Indicator. It will never erupt over the top due to the special shape of the land below it and it generates static electricity.

'Henry is old school. He only delivers static electricity to the twin Slava Slopes and the twin Hot Spots in small portioned boxes and only when he wants to. They then have to make it flow and make it work for their manufacturing processors. By doing that he holds control.

'Molly from the twin Slava Slopes and Pete and Peg from the twin Hot Spots have been eternally fighting him to do things differently but he won't hear of it, he just gets more and more stubborn.'

Will and Pat looked at each other as they remembered that Jack was the sonnic of Molly and Max was the sonnic of Pete and Peg.

'Do Hillary and Henry have any famnic at all?'

'They had a daugnic but she died. It was around that time that Henry changed to horrid Henry. Hillary simply went along with him. They no longer attended any events and they refused to do things differently from the way they were doing them. Henry became impossible to negotiate with and he insisted Hillary do what he wanted as well. No nicbeing knows exactly what happened.'

'What about the ven-la-rocs?' asked Will. 'How do they fit in up here?'

'What is a ven-la-roc?' asked Hugh.

Reece grabbed Hugh's wrist and squeezed it. 'I'll show you later.' She winked at him then looked down towards her pockets.

'You got that?' enquired Marky as he pointed at Reece.

'Yep all fine here, please go ahead,' she politely responded.

'Ven-la-rocs are like medicine that we can eat. They help injuries to repair, they make us feel better when we're sick and most of all they stop nicbeings from dehydrating. As you've probably felt there is no relief in the temperature here and it's easy to dehydrate if we don't get enough steam. The alternative is find water ha ha ha,' he said, tongue in cheek. 'It would be easier to blast water out of this dry surface than to get hold of the ven-la-rocs and we all know blasting water is impossible.'

'What do these ven-la-rocs taste like?' asked Hugh.

'They are tasteless, but they rehydrate us instantly and they keep us healthy. There were far fewer deaths when the ven-la-rocs were free flowing.'

'They used to be easily accessible?'

'Yes they were, way back when Hillary first discovered how to make them. They're her recipe, you see. Hillary is a clever libnic but she's married to an extremely greedy aquanic; they won't even answer their door if we knock begging for help. In fact their door has been locked for so long I'm sure it no longer functions as a door.'

'It's amazing how one nicbeing can control the whole of the planet even down to the finest detail of exactly how much electricity you can have when you're producing. It's absurd!'

'Sure is Pat; it's so hard to fathom and I live here. Where are you all from anyway?'

'Pat and my friend Amy who is lost and I are from Earth. Amy and I are human and Pat is a dog,' answered Will.

'Reece and I are from Mercury,' piped up Hugh.

'You do mean the planet Mercury? If so, you're a long way from home.'

'We sure are. I am an ironkidcaptron and my sistron Reece which is sisnic for you is a rockkidgemtron. Basically I'm made of iron and Reece is made of rock.'

Marky made a gesture with his hand indicating to look at him. 'Just as I'm made of lava.'

'Yes,' agreed Hugh.

'What happened to the other one? Did you say Amy was her name?'

'Yes,' responded Will very definitely as anger surged inside of him. 'She was with Hugh and suddenly she was gone.'

'You're suggesting she's been taken? Or got lost?'

'We have no idea Marky; have you got any clues for us?' probed Pat.

'This may sound strange but I did spot another stranger rather like Will. Will is much better looking but this one looked the same age. He was pretty grubby. I spotted him and I thought he may have been the one riding in the large lavalorry that cracked the wall so I headed toward him but there were too many spectators so I didn't get near him. Then I saw him take off.'

'Did he have anyone with him?'

'I saw him dragging the hand of someone who may have been human but I was not close enough to see any detail. My view was blocked.'

Will turned to Pat. 'That's the second time we've heard there's another human here. I wonder why whoever it was would take Amy? How would they know she was here?'

'That's what we need to find out,' said Pat. 'Marky, just before the last of the Date Wall goes down, what are those humps at the top and the different shaped stones where each of the humps meets?'

'There are thirteen humps in total and where each hump meets that indicates a month. You need thirteen humps to have twelve meeting points. Venus is Earth's twin and although a day on Venus is approximately 243 Earth days because we rotate so much more slowly than Earth and in the opposite direction, but we pretend we have twelve months. You can also notice on this side of the wall where the libnic is etched in, each meeting point has a different shaped amethyst stone. Where the second and the third hump meet there is a heart shape but there's no stone in that one.'

'You're right Marky, I didn't notice the stone missing until you pointed it out,' commented Will. 'Is it the same on the other side where the aquanic is etched in?'

'The shapes are there but the stones are not. When the wall was erected we found only eleven different shaped amethysts. None of them was of any quality; they are riddled with faults and their violet colour is very weak but the shapes fitted perfectly into the wall. It was one of Mother Nature's gifts to us and it made our wall very decorative on one side.'

'So Marky, let me get this straight. Both sides have the shapes etched in but only one side has eleven of the twelve stones.'

'Right.'

'What did you do then?'

'That's how I got my name. My job is to place a MARK between the humps to indicate what month we should be in. It is more for entertainment than anything else.'

Reece giggled.

'How do you know so much about Earth?' asked Pat.

'I only know about Earth and Venus being twins and that Earth has twelve months. My famnic are the only nicbeings that have ever run the Date Wall. It's our job.'

'What are you going to do now it's sunk into the ground?'

Marky watched sadly at the last piece of the Date Wall went down. 'I really don't know. Now, getting to the twin Slava Slopes, the twin Hot Spots, vennis and Wasteland and even the Lava Hi House is going to be impossible as we can no longer use this land. The Date Wall marked the middle of this territory on Venus.'

Will was deep in thought. 'I think I've worked something out. Marky, you mentioned that Venus and Earth are twins, right?'

'Yes.'

'I've learnt that so I agree. Here you have twin Slava Slopes, twin Hot Spots and just one Lava Hi House.'

'Yes and we had just one Date Wall.'

'I can understand there being one Lava Hi House based purely on the originality of the shape of the land underneath it but I wonder if there was ever two Date Walls. Is it possible there is another one somewhere?'

Marky laughed so hard Will was shocked. 'You think we have a spare Date Wall hanging around somewhere in case the one we have got sucked into the ground?'

'I don't know but it's not entirely impossible.'

'Here's the deal, Will. You played a part in the first one sinking. Do you agree?'

Will went to protest but Marky held up his hand. 'Granted there were circumstances but you did play a part.'

'I'll agree on those terms.'

'Okay, if you find a way to assemble another Date Wall, I will engage every nicbeing I know on this planet to stop what they're doing and dig every inch of it to find Amy.'

'Marky, did you say the word, assemble?

'Yeah.'

Will looked to Pat then back to Marky. 'Do you really mean that?'

'I really do. The Date Wall is my life. It's part of me and I want to hand it down to my childnics.'

Will was thrilled with the challenge of the rebuild but even more excited at the prospect of finding Amy.

'Okay so now that is sorted, I have something that may help you.'

They all watched on as Marky jogged to another lavalorry and pulled out a small tile sized flat sheet of solid lava. He ran back and handed it to Will.

'What is this?'

'The aquanic image is on one side and the libnic image on the other side. These are exact replicas of the images that were on the Date Wall. Keep that lava tile safe because I want it back. It's no ordinary tile! You'll need it in case you're able to honour your side of the deal.'

'Thanks Marky, it's the perfect size. It fits in the palm of my hand.'

'I hope it will be me who thanks you soon.'

Pat moved to see the lava tile. 'While I admire Will's enthusiasm I do have to be the voice of reason. In the event we're not able to find or reassemble the Date Wall what are the repercussions?'

'There is a risk involved in everything. Right now, I do not know what the risk is. Venus is in dire straits. Henry is fighting for total control of all industry on this planet because he hates change. Our pride and joy, the Date Wall, has been sucked into a sinkhole half assisted, half a natural disaster. Our nicbeings are forced to cross the planet, weaving around volcanos, which will take them twice as long and slow our activities and industries right down. Is that enough repercussions for you?'

'I guess so,' agreed Pat.

'I also know Henry will have no problem firing as many burning lava rocks as needed in any direction to get his own way.'

'What do the nicbeings do to fire back at him?'

'That's the problem Hugh. Not a damn thing. He has gotten away with it for so long, the nicbeings work around it. Venus is the planet for love, and we're hoping someday Henry will acquire some.'

'That's a little naïve, don't you think?'

'Probably Hugh, but that's how it is at the moment.'

'Marky, we will need some tools or at least some pointers as to where to get materials to build with,' said Will.

'First stop the twin Hot Spots; they are where the material and tool nicbeings work. To get there you will need to weave behind the volcano at the Wasteland, around the back of the twin Slava Slopes and continue on to the Hot Spots. There used to be access from where we are to the twin Hot Spots but the sinkhole has changed that so you need to go all the way around.'

Will was keen to get going. 'Marky, how will we contact you if we need you?'

'The two way of course.'

Will nodded and then held out his hand. 'Thank you.'

'No, thank you,' Marky said as they shook hands then they all bade one another farewell and Marky took off into the devastated crowd.

'We've got a gigantic task in front of us but we need to map out a clear picture so let's all climb up onto Will's lorry,' said Pat.

Will grabbed Pat and whispered, 'I keep telling you when there's a Will there's a way.'

'Don't go getting ahead of yourself,' replied Pat as they climbed on the lorry when Will mentioned, 'The most important thing is, we think Amy's been taken.'

71

'OMG!' exclaimed Hugh. 'I can't believe I forgot to give you this earlier!' He pulled out Amy's ring and held it up.

Will's eyes widened as a ray of light came up from the ground through the ring and sent a single ray in the direction of the Lava Hi House, the twin Slava Slopes and the twin Hot Spots. There was no single ray in the direction of the Wasteland. They all stared as the rays dissipated.

'That was amazing,' said Will, taking the ring Hugh held out.

'I think it was trying to tell us something,' suggested Pat.

Will held the ring up and looked through it again, recalling the conversation they'd had on the way there with Amy. 'Pat, do you remember what Amy called this ring?'

Pat thought for a while and at the same time both he and Will said, 'The ring of calmness.'

'Our mission as given to us by Cyril was G, Generate the Ring of Calmness,' reminded Will.

'That's great, but that was letter G. We have a larger task right now of A, assemble the "new" Date Wall. The best part is we have no clue if such a thing exists.'

'To the twin Hot Spots we go,' commanded Will with Reece by his side and Pat and Hugh following in their lorries behind.

CHAPTER SEVEN
DESOLATE DATEWALL
AND AMY

'Will, it's one thing that we're heading to the twin Hot Spots but what are we going to do when we get there? Over.'

'This is an outside shot Pat, but I'm hoping to run into our vennis buddy Max. It was mentioned that his famnic Pete and Peg own it. Maybe they'll know how to assist with tools and materials for building. Over.'

'I'm nervous that you made a deal to find and or assemble a Date Wall in a land where we have no assistance, no materials and no tools, in exchange for finding Amy. That could take us an eternity. Over.'

'We should be grateful that time on Earth stands still while we're here. The show we were volunteers in will be right at the part we left it. Over.'

Pat sighed as Will came back on.

'Plus, it's hard enough steering through these mounds of rocks in this wasteland, and we're too far in to go back now. Over,' said Will. He turned his head to see Pat and Hugh behind him and noticed the same mound of rocks he had noticed when they were hoisted up in the vennis vacket. 'Change of route everyone. Follow me. Over,' said Will as he veered his lorry off the beaten track and to the foot of a large pile of rocks.

They got out of their lorries and stood staring in silence at the pile in front of them. Will bent down and tried to free one rock. Hugh lent a hand until they had it free and lying on the ground. Will stared at it, deep in concentration.

'What is it Will?' asked Hugh.

'When we were active in the vennis game I noticed this pile of lava rocks. They are all the same shape which is very unusual.'

Pat, Hugh and Reece agreed.

'What really caught my eye apart from the similar shape on each one was the etching. Let's turn this over.' They did so, and Will added, 'See, there is etching on both sides.'

Pat moved in for a closer look. 'So there is.'

Will pulled the small tile that Mark had given him from his pocket and held the magnifier in front of it. A magnified image of the aquanic came up in it.

'Pat, this part of the image at the bottom of the tile matches the etching on this lava rock. We may have just found the Date Wall that needs to be assembled.'

'Wait up there Will,' said Pat as he lifted his paw into the air. 'Granted this one rock is showing similarities, but we need to be sure there are enough matching lava rocks here to make a wall.'

'You want to know what I don't like about you, Pat?'

'What could that be?'

'I don't like that you get your facts together first. It's annoying that you think it through.'

'We could always do things the other way and bask in our own glory that could result in disappointment.'

'Could.'

'Could not also,' countered Pat. 'Hurry up Will. Get on with it; how do you want to do this?'

Will considered. 'Now that we think we've found the material that needs assembling, we still need equipment and tools.'

'With luck the twin Hot Spots will help with that.'

'Exactly, Hugh,' answered Will then he went silent.

'Can I assist you?' asked Reece.

'You?' said Will. 'Do you know what to do?'

'Well, I'm not Amy but you'd be surprised at what Amy has taught me; for example I know you work so well as a team because you are the logistics man and she gathers all the tools for you to do it.'

'You've been paying attention,' said Will.

'I usually do you know. Now let's be clear... I'm not Amy, but I have made one observation.'

Pat asked, 'What is it Reece?'

'We think we have the pieces for the wall but we don't have a site to build on. It's apparent we can't assemble it here as the land is uneven and filled with waste and stacks of lava rocks.'

'That's a fair observation.'

'I've thought of something, too,' said Hugh. 'If these end up being the right rocks, how are we going to stick them all together?'

'I have something to add,' put in Pat. 'How many of the same shaped rocks are here and how many do we need?'

By this time Will was bent down on one knee with head in his hands.

'Come on Will, it's not that bad.'

'No it's not, and here's the plan. Let's continue to the twin Hot Spots and see if the nicbeings there have a solution to move these rocks. From there we can come back via the twin Slava Slopes which is en-route and check out what they do. With luck we can ride on the Mosaic Moveator, then get back here to move the rocks in search of a site to build.'

'Sounds feasible Will but I've got another idea. Time is of the essence and the sooner we find Amy the better and now we think we've found the new Date Wall rocks we don't want to lose them. Hugh, you alter Amy's lavalorry to have a tray at the back instead of seats, then together you and Reece can load these rocks onto the back of it. Will and I will continue to the twin Hot Spots in search of machinery or tools or anything we think we may need.'

'That sounds like a better plan than mine, Pat.'

'I hope you don't mind,' said Pat.

'Not at all.'

'A few more things, Hugh and Reece...Please pay attention to how many rocks you're loading and check they have some form of etching on both sides.'

'Shall do,' responded Reece as Hugh took off to alter the lavalorry.

As Reece turned to follow Hugh, Pat brushed his paw against the back of her hand so she looked at him. 'Remember, the best laid plans can come undone, but let's give it a try.'

'Sure thing Pat,' she answered as she held her thumb to the air.

Pat and Will got back in their lavalorries and headed for the twin Hot Spots.

'Get me out of here! Who are you and what do you want?' screamed Amy, frantically trying to free herself from the clutches of her kidnapper. 'Get this bag off my head. I can't see or breathe.' She squirmed harder. 'Who are you and what do you want?' she screamed and jabbed her elbow hoping to hit the kidnapper in some private area.

She sure is a fighter, thought the kidnapper.

'Not long now,' was all she heard. She could not recognise the voice.

Amy continued to struggle as the kidnapper pushed her head down and dragged her on her knees through what felt like a confined space.

'Take it easy. I can't see where I'm going and I'm crawling as fast as I can,' she yelled. 'Can you hear or are you deaf? I can't see and you're pulling my arm from its socket. I'm going as fast as I can, so take it easy.'

'Go faster,' was all she heard as she continued being dragged and often fell from her knees to her stomach.

Finally they crawled out of the confined area and the bag was ripped from her head. She looked around. It was very dark but faint light seeped through, enough for Amy to be able to stare at the human in front of her. He was shorter than Will with light brown hair, a mean looking face and mole on the top of his left cheek. He was overweight and dressed in jeans with a dirty khaki tee-shirt. In fact he was filthy all over.

Amy was scared but determined to return to Will and Pat safely. 'Who are you?' she yelped

The boy laughed out loud. 'As if you don't know who I am!'

'Should I?'

'I would say although you may not know what I looked like, I'm sure you've heard of me. You took my place.'

'What?'

'If you can't guess who I am, I'm sure you've heard of my pact... and by the way, I hate you for replacing me.'

'You're Zac? Will's old friend?'

'It took you longer than I expected it would to work me out.'

77

'Don't flatter yourself; you're not the first thought in my mind.'

Zac's face filled with anger. 'What are you doing on Venus, Amy?'

'Shouldn't I be asking you that question?'

A loud bolt of thunder vibrated the room they were in. It scared Amy so much she was shaking.

'So this is little Amy, Will's precious friend.'

'How do you know my name?'

'I made it my business to learn all about you once I found out you are now Will's best friend.'

'It's not my fault something happened between you two. I didn't even know Will at the time that happened.'

'Doesn't matter Amy Spurt,' said Zac in a condescending voice. 'I've had you marked for a long time and now I finally have you.'

'What have I got that you could possibly want?'

'Now where should I start?' questioned Zac as he walked slowly around her in the small room.

No wonder it is so dark in here. This room is so small, she thought.

'You're going to show me a thing or two on how to dig for amethyst stones in this volcano-filled land and more importantly how to get the magnifier out of Will's clutches.'

Amy knew what she'd heard was completely ridiculous.

'Firstly Zac, I don't know a thing of where to start to dig for amethysts. I don't know what you've heard about the magnifier but it only works in the right hands and Will is the only one with the right hands.'

'That's not entirely true Amy, it has the power to destroy in the wrong hands and that's my reason for wanting it.'

'Go your hardest with that Zac. Will is very protective of it.'

'That was apparent on Mercury when he lost it just after he'd arrived there.'

'Have you ever heard the saying, Learn from your mistakes?'

'That's not the Will I know, the Will I know follows whatever I suggest.'

'That may have been the case in the past but it's not true of him now.'

'I don't think so Amy.'

'What are you doing here on Venus anyway?'

'You've obviously not heard of my role here. You mean Cyril clean forgot to tell you?'

'Tell me what exactly?'

'I keep telling Henry, Cyril is a waste of time; he's too old.'

'Hasn't anyone taught you to respect your elders?'

'No. They should respect me.'

'I suppose you're the human that works for Henry?'

'You're smarter than I thought Amy Spurt,' he said.

He was so close she felt the spit from his mouth hit the side of her head.

Amy eyeballed him. 'What do you do, feed his insatiable greed?'

Zac snapped, 'What has Will said about me?'

'Will thought you were a cool guy but it's apparent you've changed! What exactly is it that you do for Henry?'

'We're going to take over this planet, one twin act at a time.'

'Twin act?'

'First we'll destroy the twin Hot Spots and then the twin Slava Slopes. All the nicbeings that wish to cooperate will be employed. The ones that won't will be banished to the wasteland to live amongst all the dirt and the mounds of rock and limited steam. The best part is Will involuntarily assisted with tearing down of the Date Wall.' Zac laughed.

'What's so funny?'

'All the nicbeings will be blaming him. That's the price you pay for always having the best and being the best at everything.'

Amy's eyes shot open. 'You're jealous of him.'

'Not jealous. Green with envy. Everything always falls into place for Will. He gets what he wants, kids always want to be friends with him at school, and he is the chosen one for space adventures.'

'You've got some of that wrong Zac.'

'The Will I know always got what he wanted.'

'Is that what this is all about? You're siding with Henry the most evil aquanic on Venus just to get back at Will?'

'We'll prevent all you do-gooders from finding calming solutions by promoting turmoil and chaos that will lead the nicbeings to fight against each other. Bring on the fire and the weapons and anything it takes to stop Will from proving our pact.'

'Why don't you join Will on the quest rather than hinder him?'

'I would if the magnifier was given to me. Even when we were friends his stuff was always better than mine and it was me who got him interested in space in the first place.' Zac hardened his expression, stuck out his chest and crossed his arms.

Amy had never met anyone like Zac. She was petrified by his envy.

'Apart from the fact you want to use me as bait to lure Will, what makes you think I know how to dig for amethysts and what do you want them for anyway?'

'They're valuable here. Only two large stones have ever been found. If you don't do as I say, the CHAMJAN will never arrive to pick you up as your mission won't be complete. Will and that stupid dog of yours will be stuck here.'

The hairs on the back of Amy's neck rose. She couldn't bear anyone speaking ill of Pat or Will, so she said, 'Okay, what do you want me to do?'

'I knew you'd see it my way, but it took more convincing than I bargained for.'

Zac had kept his hand on his pocket and every so often whatever was in that pocket vibrated.

'What have you got in your pocket?'

'It's my message machine.'

'Who could be messaging you? I mean how do they know where you are and how would the message get through these walls?'

'Henry, the ruler of Venus, messages me.'

'Ha, as if Henry is the ruler, and he's so out of touch, how can he string a message together?'

Zac hesitated. 'He maybe a little older but his messages are clear. You can read can't you Amy?'

'Trying to put me down and belittle me is not going to work Zac. I know you're a bully... well at least your mother is. Obviously it's rubbed off on you.'

'Well, well, well, Will's found himself a feisty one here. Is there anything he hasn't told you?'

'Regardless of what you think Will is a very loyal friend.'

'What about our pact Amy? Has he told you about that?'

'What do you think? I just told you Will was loyal, so you work it out.'

'I'll find out if you're lying to me.'

'Why would I, where's the gain? That's your way of handling things, not mine.'

Zac did not respond, but Amy wanted some answers. 'What's the matter? Has the cat got your tongue?'

He again did not respond.

'What do you want with me anyway?'

'Apart from being Will's best friend you cannot work out why we would want to kidnap you?'

'We? Oh, of course, you're Henry's slave. It's not possible for him to do his own dirty work.'

That comment made Zac mad so he threw his fist into the air. 'You're not doing yourself any favours.'

Amy looked at her tied up hands and noticed her ring was missing.

No, she thought as her heart sank. *My ring of calmness has gone.* 'Where are we Zac?'

'In my secret shelter under the surface of Venus.'

'This is your own shelter? How often do you come here?'

'Whenever I want.'

'You mentioned Henry sends you messages; how do you get them?'

'It's magic. I just get them on my message machine,' he said as he spread his fingers apart in the air.

'What do you do when you're not receiving messages?'

'Run the tasks I've been assigned like set the lava rocks on fire and shoot them into flying lavalorries.'

'That was you who did that to Will? I could kill you for that! He could have been hurt.'

Zac nodded proudly. 'The best part is that it worked.'

Amy looked away. 'How long are you going to keep me here?'

'As long as it takes for Will to surrender the magnifier.'

Amy laughed so hard she couldn't stop herself. 'What are you going to do to get Will to surrender?'

'Amy you look smart but you ask some dumb questions. Why do you think I've got you?'

'Will won't surrender the magnifier.'

'He's not much of a friend if he's not willing to give up a silly magnifier for the safety of his best friend now is he?'

Amy looked around this dullish room. It was small, circular in shape and was stuffy. She was sure not much air got in but was unsure how she got in there.

'Don't you get dehydrated down here Zac?'

'I don't stay down long enough but you will if you don't do as I say.'

'You're using me to get to Will. He probably doesn't know where I am or how to get to me. I don't even know how I got here.'

'Good, let's leave it that way.'

'Since we both agree I have no idea how to get out can you untie my wrists? The ties are cutting my circulation. I'm not much good to use as bait if I've got no circulation.'

Zac was not keen but agreed and did so.

'How do you intend to destroy the twin Hot Spots and the twin Slava Slopes?' went on Amy.

'The same way we destroy everything, with burning lava rocks. No structure will withstand the onslaught we have planned.'

'You really don't have much love in you do you?'

'I love blasting and destroying things.

'I'm pretty sure that's not the sort of love I'm talking about.'

'I love the fact I caught you and you're stuck.'

'Yep, that's not it either.'

'They are my types of love.'

Amy was tiring of the conversation but just then Zac received a message and next thing she knew he took off and left her alone in the stuffy dull room.

Amy sat on the ground with folded legs and rubbed her eyes. *How did I get here and what has happened to my ring?* she asked herself.

CHAPTER EIGHT
MOVEMENT FROM
ALL SIDES

'Get up here Zac, I told you when you work for me and I call you have to be here instantly.'

Zac panted as he bolted two at a time the many stairs in the Lava Hi House trying to reach Henry.

'Zac,' Henry yelled, 'I can't see you.'

'I'm here Henry,' he said, barely able to get the words out as he put his hand on his hip and bent over trying to catch his breath.

'Where have you been?'

'Doing as you asked. You told me to capture Amy and I have.'

'Where is she?'

'Locked up in the cavity under the sinkhole as per your instructions.'

'Ah yes, I'm a genius for creating that sinkhole. It was by far my best achievement yet, and, the nicbeings think it was a natural disaster. Couple that with my expert lava rock shot that caused that over-sized lavalorry to crack the wall and you get the result. Genius, genius, I'm a genius.'

Zac stood listening to Henry praise himself. He admired Henry and would do anything for him. 'You are a genius Henry!' he agreed.

'Now the Date Wall is down, we have that human locked up and the nicbeings have to travel over mountainous terrain to get to the twin Slava Slopes for steam. Otherwise they have to beg me for ven-la-rocs.

It's the only way they'll survive. Chaos is brewing. It's fabulous... just fabulous.'

'What about the spades and shovels and lava bullets that keep getting pelted at Hi House?'

'I've enlisted my army of nicbeings who would usually deliver the boxes of static electricity to stop delivering and start fighting back. They'll sort out those silly shovels, spades and pellets.' Henry turned to where Zac was standing. 'Watch and learn, son, watch and learn. You will see soon how quickly everything is about to change.'

'What are you going to do?'

'Oh Zac—' Henry stopped mid-sentence.

Zac could see he had become fixated on something.

'What is it Henry?' Zac walked up beside where Henry was sitting to see what had caught his attention. 'What are you looking at?'

Henry hopped up and peered through his large binoculars that were built into the middle of the top floor of the Lava Hi House. They were generally used to pinpoint areas where problems may have occurred. 'Ahhhhh,' was all Henry said.

'What can you see?'

'That boy... the one like you, and that four legged thing... what do you call them again?'

'Dogs, Henry.'

'Yes that boy and the dog just went behind the twin Slava Slopes. It looks as if they're heading for the twin Hot Spots.'

Zac stood listening with widened eyes.

'What business do they want there I wonder?' said Henry.

Zac became nervous. When Henry used that tone of voice it usually meant another attack was imminent.

'What are you going to do?'

'Why are they here sticking their noses in?'

'Cyril sent them, you know.'

Henry turned to Zac with anger in his eyes. 'Don't you dare speak to me like that.'

'Sorry sir, but it's true.'

'Do you think I don't know that?'

'Henry, for goodness sake, what is going on up there? You haven't stopped screaming,' complained Hillary, popping her head in.

'You just mind your own business,' snarled Henry. 'I'm trying, but your screaming is thumping through me. My lava is starting to crack.'

'I always knew you were cracking up Hillary,' said Henry and for the first time a slight smirk came across his face.

'You're the one that's cracked up. Have you seen yourself lately?'

Hillary was right. Henry's body of lava was very worn, and age had a lot to do with it.

'What are you going to do Henry?' Zac asked again nervously.

'It's time we brought the mining industry to a halt.'

'You're going to destroy the twin Hot Spots?'

'Not me, boy; we. We're a team.'

Zac smiled at the implied compliment.

'Now Hugh, I'm the best at this since it was me who suggested we put holes in the pipe on Mercury. I think I know the way to work these lava rocks out.'

Hugh didn't take too well to his little sistron telling him what to do. 'I'm the ironkidcaptron here. I'll work it out.'

Reece figured she would let Hugh lead the project. 'Okay then. How many rocks do we need for the bottom layer of the wall?'

Hugh stood there with a blank look. 'Do you know?'

'Not exactly, but I could take a guess.'

'All right,' said Hugh in a disbelieving tone, 'how many?'

'My guess is thirteen.'

Hugh really was baffled. 'Where did you get that number from?'

'Remember when the Date Wall was going down? I think it was Pat that asked Marky what the humps were at the top of the wall. Marky said there were thirteen and it has something to do with the months of the year on Earth.'

'That may be true, but they also mentioned there were twelve months of the year on Earth.'

'Yes, but a month is only counted where the two humps meet. So if you want twelve meeting points you need thirteen humps.'

'You win on this occasion.'

'Thank you Hugh,' said Reece, very proud of herself. 'By the way, did you remember to get the tile with the etched images of the aquanic and libnic from Will before he left?'

'I clean forgot.'

'Me too.'

'Oh well. I think I have a vague recollection of what we are looking for plus we don't have anything to put between the rocks to hold them together. With luck, Will and Pat will return with such a thing.'

'I'm fairly sure we're a long way off needing stuff to stick the Date Wall together. Right now we need to secure the rocks.'

'Got that. So we need to search for thirteen humps to get a good start.'

'Absolutely. Come over here and help lift this rock. I think a hump rock is wedged underneath it.'

Hugh and Reece worked side by side and stacked the whole thirteen semi circled hump-shaped rocks onto the back of the lavalorry.

'There are lots of lavalorries heading out this way and stirring up dust. They look to be all making their own paths,' said Reece. 'I wonder where they're going?'

Hugh looked at Reece with a blank expression. 'You didn't really mean to ask that question. Please tell me you were talking out loud to yourself.'

'Why?'

'The reason so many lavalorries are passing is because they need steam from the boiling lava that slides down the twin Slava Slopes. Without the roads around the Date Wall the nicbeings have no other option.'

'Okay, so I had a temporary memory loss.'

Hugh stared at her. 'Please make sure those moments don't happen too often.'

'Ha ha,' Reece retaliated.

'Speaking of which, you pointed out the bulge in your pocket of ven-la-rocs but you never did get around to sharing them with me. Can I have one?'

'Sure Hugh; here you go.'

Hugh inspected the ven-la-roc before placing it in his mouth. As Reece looked at him she felt she too should indulge as the task ahead was arduous.

'What do you think?' she asked.

'They are really yummy and I feel great now I've had one. Breathing is perfect and energy has been boosted. What about you Reece?'

'Same, except I still feel sad about Amy being lost.'

'Don't worry. We'll find her.'

'I just hope she's not hurt.'

'Me too.'

Hugh was devastated about Amy missing but didn't want to show his feelings so he changed the topic very quickly. 'Let's get to work sorting, carrying and stacking these rocks onto the lavalorry before the others get back.'

'Wow Pat, look at all these lavalorries. It's like the main street of a big city in the middle of the day, Over.'

'This is the livelihood of Venus, so it is the main street of a big city. The main thoroughfare has turned into a pool of boiling lava so what else do you expect the nicbeings to do? Over.'

'Exactly what they're doing I guess. Over.'

'Remember, they survive on steam so they are doing the best they can to get to the twin Slava Slopes to stock up. Over.'

'I wonder why Henry is so hellbent on keeping everything the same? Over.'

'Funnily enough it is often how change comes about. Over.'

'What do you mean by that, Pat? Over.'

'Watch out!' screamed Pat. Will had nearly caused an accident because he was concentrating on talking to Pat on the two way.

'Phew, lucky you saw that lorry. I nearly ran into it. Over.'

'Mmmmmm,' was all Pat replied.

'Anyway Pat, you were telling me how change comes about. Over.'

'Oh yeah, in some countries on planet Earth the people have had to protest and fight the government for changes to occur. Change is something most people do not like. Over.'

'Do you think that is what is happening here? The nicbeings are fighting the government, which is Henry, for change? Over.'

'Henry has control over the two most sought after resources; the ven-la-rocs which aid dehydration which is like medicine here with this climate and static electricity which if used in the right way and is harnessed to flow would open countless opportunities. Over.'

'Pat you're so clever, I've been trying to work out what this fight is about and it is a fight between a government and its people or in this case it's nicbeings. Over.'

Pat and Will giggled.

'Let's cut out saying over at the end of each sentence. We know we're talking to each other across the two way.'

'Roger that Pat.'

'What about the other one like you that we've heard about!'

'That freaks me out,' said Will.

'Why?'

'I've thought a lot about that also and even though I have no idea how this could possibly be I'm wondering if the other one like me is Zac!'

'You mean your friend from way back? How did you come to that conclusion?'

'I can't quite put my finger on it but there are two things you should know about him. Firstly he is obsessed with space. It was he who got me interested.

Secondly, he got really envious of anyone who got something he didn't.'

'So you're saying he was envious of you?'

'I never thought he was envious of me; he was an only child so got everything he wanted. If anything I should have been envious of him.'

'So why do you think the other human here is Zac?'

'Because of Amy going missing. I don't know how he would know Amy but I do wonder if he is jealous that I now have another best friend and she's a girl.'

Pat stared into thin air.

'I know it's a stab in the dark and there's probably no truth to it,' said Will.

'You might be onto something. Park near the other lavalorries now. We've made it to the twin Hot Spots.'

Pat and Will alighted from their lavalorries and walked through a door in the side of one of the twin Hot Spots volcanos. It was marked *staff entrance* so they hoped they would run into a nicbeing able to help them.

'Excuse me, excuse me,' screamed a libnic, shuffling towards them from the other side of the volcano.

Pat and Will looked around at the flurry of activity. Many holes had been dug and piles and piles of sand and rock lay beside them. Nicbeings, both aqua and libnics, assisted each other with their tasks as lavalorries moved around taking materials from area and delivering them to another. The movement and the noise were fascinating.

'I could stand and watch this scene for some time,' said Will.

'Look at how they manually use their machines. See what I mean when I say Venus could advance so far if only the electricity were free flowing? They have it, but it's not being used to its potential, thanks to Henry.'

'Excuse me,' the libnic voice sounded again, but this time she was beside them. She was very short and looked as wide as she was tall. Will had to look down and Pat only needed to slightly adjust his head.

'Hello, I'm Will,' Will said as he lowered his hand, making her able to reach it.

The libnic did not shake hands but rather took a step back staring up at Will then down at Pat. Her facial expression seemed astonished.

Will looked at Pat, not sure where to from here so Pat piped up. 'Hello ma'am.'

This time she stood staring at Pat until an aquanic joined the group.

'What's happening here Peg?'

'Oh Pete, what is that? I've never seen anything like it.'

Pat rolled his eyes, having almost forgot how novel he was on these planets.

'Peggy dear, I don't really know.' Pete looked at Will. 'What is it?'

'He's an animal known as a dog from planet Earth. His name is Pat and he talks so he understands what you're asking.'

'Hello, I'm Pat,' said Pat as he held his paw up to Pete.

A little slow off the mark, Pete held out his hand and shook Pat's paw. 'Nice to meet you.'

Peg who was standing beside Pete said, 'what about me? I need to meet him.'

Pat graciously held his paw up to Peg and shook her hand. 'Hello; Peg, is it?'

'Yes, and how lovely to meet you,' she answered then continued, 'Would you mind if I pat you Pat?'

They all shared a laugh at that comment.

'Go right ahead. I love being patted.'

Pete looked at Will. 'And you are...?'

'Oops sorry sir. I temporarily forgot my manners. My name is Will and I also come from planet Earth.'

'I'm Pete and this is my wifenic Peg whom you have just met. Now what can we do for you?'

'We're working on a small project and wanted to see if we could borrow some tools.'

'Paanic, Paanic,' screamed a voice from the other side of the volcano.

Pete looked around to see Max running toward him. 'What is it Max?'

'They were our valls in the game I played of vennis earlier with Jack.'

'These two?' Pete looked puzzled as he held his index and middle fingers up pointing at Will and Pat.

'Yes, it was definitely them. There are more of them.' Max stood there nodding at his paanic and maanic. 'They were so much fun. It was the best game of vennis ever. Even Jack said so.'

Pete turned to Will and Pat. 'It's looks like my sonnic is a fan of yours.' He turned back to Max. 'Have you met Will and Pat?'

'We didn't meet. We just played.'

Will and Pat introduced themselves to Max as Peg stood up from patting Pat. 'Pete, why don't you and Max show Will and Pat around the twin Hot Spots?'

'Why don't we?' added Pete as he looked at Will and Pat.

'That sounds great.'

'Come in my lavalorry, Will,' screamed Max. He tore off and brought his lavalorry to where they were standing.

'Max, we will all get in with you.'

'Okay Paanic.'

Off they went for their own exclusive tour of the twin Hot Spots.

CHAPTER NINE
PETE'S PIT

Max drove them over mounds of rocks then on a flat pathway beside large holes. They crossed several more large mounds then traversed more flat pathways skirting the large holes.

'Want to see down the mine, Will?' Max asked.

Before Will could answer Max drove the lavalorry right beside a deep bottomless hole, causing rocks to roll down into it. Will shuddered, because he was on the side closest to the hole.

'Want to see another one Will?'

Max drove the lorry this time even closer so the back wheel skidded into it. Fortunately the other three wheels were strong enough to get them back on track.

Pete could see Will was not coping, and he said, 'Max, stop that.'

Max pulled the lorry up.

Will stood looking down a very deep dark hole that seemed bottomless. 'Ahhh, how do you get down there exactly?'

Pete chuckled to himself as he casually walked over to two closed sliding lava doors that looked like elevator doors. 'We take the lava lator.'

Will looked to where Pete was standing and felt instant relief.

Pat up to this point had decided being a spectator was a better option, but now he entered the conversation. 'Pete, where are we taking the lava lator to?'

'I am going to show you Pete's Pit, which is full of not so precious gems.'

'That does sound interesting.'

'Come on then.'

The lava lator arrived and all four hopped in. It was nothing more than a moving platform with no walls around that descended into a deep shaft. The lower they went the more the light faded until they were in complete darkness.

'Sorry about the lack of light. With limited electricity we have to save it when we can. There's no other way to describe Henry than mean,' said Pete.

As they alighted from the lava lator dim lighting appeared.

'Paanic, they probably don't even know who Henry is,' put in Max.

'You have a short memory. We were flung there after you played vennis.'

Pete looked sternly at Max. 'Max, I don't recall you mentioning that part.'

A wave of guilt washed over Will for mentioning something he shouldn't have.

Max nervously answered, 'It wasn't me; it was Jack.'

'You two make me angry. I've told you both before to leave Henry alone and every time you get up on those vackets you do all you can to annoy him. You do realise the more you frustrate him, the harder he makes it for us. Why can't you just stop?'

'Sorry Paanic,' said Max.

Pete shook his head. 'Young aquanics; they'll never learn.'

'Sorry Pete, I shouldn't have said anything.'

'It's fine. He knows better.'

Will patted Max on the back and mouthed the word, 'sorry.'

Max went to return the gesture and accidently ran his hand over the magnifier in Will's back pocket. 'What have you got in your pocket Will?'

Without thinking Will pulled the magnifier out and showed it to Max. 'It's my trusty magnifier.'

Max's eyes widened. Paanic,' he said in a shaky voice. 'Is that the magnifier you've told us about?'

Pete put his hand on a part of the handle Will was not holding. 'May I?'

Will looked at Pat who gave a quick nod but all other eyes were on the magnifier.

'It actually exists,' said Pete.

'Paanic, can I have a go?'

Max's beady little eyes were fixated. He could not believe this precious instrument was so close to him.

'Okay Max, but be careful. In the wrong hands that thing has the power to damage.'

'I don't have bad hands Paanic.'

'No, you don't and you won't be given the chance to prove otherwise.'

Max held it for a while longer and swung it around until Pete called time and demanded it be given back to Will, which it was. Pete then led the way to a pit where a nicbeing sat in the pit chiselling away at the sides.

'What is so special about Pete's Pit?'

Pete turned and laughed. 'Nothing really Pat. I called it Pete's Pit way before we ever started to mine and although it has produced gems none has been of any quality. How this mine works is that we have one major hole from the surface down then once we're down here we have many smaller holes. I don't know if you know but in the history of Venus only two faultless perfectly shaped amethyst rocks have been found by no other than horrid Henry. One of the rocks sits on his wifenic Hillary's finger and it's a mystery where the other one is.'

'I have a friend called Amy and she loves these amethyst stones. I didn't even know what they were until she told me.'

'Where is she now?'

'Wouldn't we all like to know! Since we've been here, Amy's been taken by someone.'

'That sounds very strange,' said Pete.

Pat was watching the aquanic in the pit. 'What has he got there Pete?'

Pete had a short conversation with the aquanic as he handed something over. Pete walked over to the light and held up the gem.

'This is the twelfth one of these amethysts that we've found. You will see it is a weak violet colour although it is a large stone and a perfectly symmetrical shape. If you look at it in the light you can see it is full of flaws.'

'If you've found so many of these, what do you do with them?' asked Pat.

'In one of our private offices there are photos of the aqua and libnics that have each found one of these stones. Every nicbeing that has found one has avoided all sorts of accidents. It's quite extraordinary. It would be fantastic if all the nicbeings that worked for me found them, because then we'd have no injuries or accidents.'

'What have you done with the actual stones once you've taken the photos and added them to the wall?'

'We made a display case that hangs on the wall beside the pictures. I had room made in it for twelve stones so now this one is found it completes that set. If any more are found I will need a new hanging display case.'

'Do you think you'll find any more?'

'I have no idea Will. I didn't think we'd find this many. Twelve is an odd number.'

Will held out his hand. 'Can I please touch it?'

'It's only fair since you shared the magnifier with us.' Pete willingly handed the amethyst over.

'This one is cone shaped. What are the shapes of the others?'

'I can't remember exactly. I think one is a square, one a triangle, and one a cylinder or something like that.' Pete looked at Max. 'Max, do you recall the shapes?'

Max shrugged. 'No. I think once we worked out they are not precious we temporarily admired them then hung them up.'

'You don't think there is anything special about them at all?'

'Not really Pat. Paanic and I are in search of precious stones. What else can we use to bargain with Henry?'

'So that is where the drive for the precious stones comes from?' said Pat.

'Yes, with faultless amethysts we'd have bargaining power with Henry but right now we have none.' Pete walked off to have a chat to another of his staff and Max followed.

Pat moved in next to Will. 'Isn't this amazing?' said Will. 'It may be full of faults but the perfect shape is something else.'

'Have any other thoughts about these twelve amethyst stones entered your head?' asked Pat.

'Aha! I've finally got it now Pat. Thank you for the prompt.'

Emergency sirens sounded suddenly and the nicbeings bolted to action. Pete instructed Will and Pat to follow him and run toward the lava lator. On the way they saw other nicbeings headed for the other lava lators and a line of them started up long lava ladders to the surface. The ground vibrated and lava rocks around started to roll. Piles of sand filled the holes. Will jumped over several rolling rocks in his haste as the vibration erupted again.

'What's happening Pete?' questioned Pat as he watched Pete drag Max into the lava lator.

'It's an emergency but I don't know what just yet.'

'Will all the nicbeings get out?'

'Hope so.'

Pete led them out of the lava lator. There were screams of terror as large boulders rolled from the top of the volcano, gathering speed as they came. They narrowly missed some of the fleeing nicbeings. Burning lava rocks came thick and fast down through the top of the twin volcanos. Will was tall enough to see a door no nicbeing was using so he put his hand through Pat's collar and ran towards it.

'Where are you dragging me?'

'Not sure Pat, but I can see an uncluttered door and I'm hoping it's an escape.'

'Is it open?' asked Pat as they arrived.

'Yes, fortunately, and there is light in here.'

They entered and the door slammed shut behind them. They immediately noticed the photos on the wall of the nicbeings that had found the non-precious but perfectly symmetrical amethysts then the display case with eleven stones in it.

'I would never normally encourage this,' said Pat, 'but grab the display case. You still have the stone that was just found? Good. See if you can get the display case off the wall. It's small enough to carry.'

Will looked sternly at Pat. 'That is stealing.'

'It is and I admire your honesty but we will tell Pete about it. I believe these stones will help with our mission and there's no time to argue.'

As Will unclipped the display cabinet from the wall, he noticed a small sack on a desk nearby so emptied the stones into it along with the one that had just been found.

'There's another door over there,' said Pat.

They went through and arrived outside the twin Hot Spots not far from where their lorries were parked. They boarded and took off amidst all the chaos.

Max came out another entrance in time to see the back of them noting they had escaped through one of the private offices.

Amy got bored sitting cross-legged, feeling sorry for herself, so hopped up and started doing cartwheels, which always made her feel better. She cartwheeled from one side of the room to the other which spanned only two cartwheels, then back again. She went back and forth until the novelty wore off.

Zac left here somehow, so there must be a way out, she thought.

Amy slipped the headband off her head as it was annoying her, then promptly put it back on. She had just remembered she had a pocket full of ven-la-rocs and a headband with the ability to shed light.

Yes, I've got this, she thought as she clapped her hands.

She engaged the headband light and then slowly shone it around the room. Indeed the room was small and very oddly shaped. She noticed a strange object shadowed in one corner, and saw it was a lava-made stool.

Zac must use this to sit on when he is stuck down here, her thoughts told her.

She grabbed the stool, moved it closer to the centre of the room then sat on it. She moved the headband to all different positions on her head and shone the light onto many different points in the room. She felt her energy swiftly drop so reached into her pocket, pulled out a ven-la-roc and planted it in her mouth. Now she felt better so she continued with shining her light, hoping to find something.

Once she had inspected the floor and the walls she decided to get off the stool and lie on the ground.

Mmmm, this ground is cool, she thought, *and that is strange.*

She then got the headband and shone the light at the ceiling, trying to make shapes with it. She held her index and middle finger in front of the light and made bunny rabbit ears for some self-entertainment. The more she did the more she laughed at herself until a sparkle from the ceiling caught her eye. She held the headband up with one hand in the position the sparkle came from then reached for the stool with the other hand. She climbed up on the stool and held the headband closer until she saw a small glimmer of purple. The roof was low enough for Amy to be able to touch once she was on the stool so she used her fingernail and scratched at it until she managed to free a larger portion of the purple colour.

Although the ground was cool the roof was the opposite and the heat emanating from it made Amy's face red. As determined as ever she continually scratched until a larger portion of the purple appeared.

There must be an easier way, she thought and then realised the heat from the light from the headband had started to turn the rock to clay.

She held the light as close as possible with one hand and kept rubbing the area with the other until finally a very large perfect symmetrically shaped amethyst appeared.

Wow! Amy could not believe what she had found. It was a perfect cylinder shape and one of the most beautiful things she had ever seen. She was so excited and couldn't believe it. All she wanted to do was to share the joy of her find with Will and Pat.

She climbed down and lay on the floor again, but this time in a different position with the headband light shining at the roof. She saw another shimmer.

Amy got up and once again melted the rock to clay to reveal a perfect square shaped amethyst. This time she was blown away and decided she was going to dig every inch of this ceiling to see how many she could find.

Zac and Henry stood side by side at the top of Lava Hi House congratulating each other on their accomplishment.

'Well done Henry. You've scared those nicbeings out of the twin Hot Spots.'

'Zaccy boy, I hope I've done more than scare them, I hope I've terrorised them out of there. Now Pete can stop whinging that his production is too slow and he does not have enough power to get more machines to dig faster.'

'Henry.'

'Yes?'

'Why are you so against the twin Hot Spots finding the amethysts?'

Henry gave Zac a filthy look. 'Are you that stupid that you don't understand? Listen up, if that Pete and Peg find amethysts bigger and as perfect as the two I've found they'll want to bargain with me for electricity and I don't want to give it to them. Right now they've got nothing I want but if they ever found such stones, I'd want them.'

'But why?' asked Zac.

'Because they're the most precious thing here. He or she that holds them is the king. Right now I'm the only one who's found them so I am the king.'

'You mentioned you have two, and I know Hillary has one, but where is the other one?' ventured Zac.

'I have it boy. Now don't ask any more questions. That topic is closed,' Henry said as he thumped his hand down on the desk in front of him.

'All ri-i-ight H-h-henry,' Zac stuttered, 'I've got it now.'

Henry turned to him. 'Good.'

Zac watched as Henry adjusted things on the desk in front of him that operated the Hi House.

'Now you have blasted the twin Hot Spots and filled in the mines, what are you going to do next?'

'Lad, have you not listening to anything I've said?'

Zac did not respond.

'Do me a favour. Take this and put the biggest red cross you can find on the door downstairs marked E/THS.'

'What is it?'

'It's red marking paint.'

Zac was too scared to ask where Henry got this paint from so he made his way down the long spiral staircase and stood in front of the E/THS door. He put the first stroke of paint on the door.

'What are you doing?'

Zac was taken by surprise, so he dropped the paint and it spilt everywhere, including all over his clothes. 'I'm....'

'Henry!' Hillary screamed from where she was standing and her voice echoed through the whole Hi House. She glared at Zac. 'Where is he?'

Zac glanced up the staircase and Hillary took off, yelling, 'Henry, what have you done?'

'Hillary you just mind your own business and go and make some ven-la-roc.'

'You old cranky aquanic, you tell me what have you done.'

'You should be happy,' retorted Henry. 'That stone on your finger is going to remain to be the largest for some time to come.'

Hillary looked out through the windows. 'What have you done? There's smoke coming out of the top of the twin Hot Spots and the nicbeings are dispersing in herds.'

'Two down and one to go,' he said to her with a smirk.

'Henry, are you that stupid? You're destroying our planet.'

'You and I both know the only way we can hold control is to keep tight reins on the ven-la-rocs and the static electricity. No other place on this planet has the indicator volcano behind them. That gives us the power.'

'We are getting old, things change—'

Henry went ballistic. 'For as long as we live things will be as they are, I don't care what the "poor little nicbeings" want, do or say. Now get back down those stairs and stick to what you're best at.'

Hillary stared at Henry and in a calm but authoritative voice said, 'Henry, we are old, and things change. Those supposed "poor little nicbeings" are going to fight back. You've controlled them, me and this planet for too long. I've let you control me because I love you but I'm sure they're sick of it. And that kid Zac... you're turning him into a monster just like yourself.'

'He was already a monster before he got here,' screamed Henry loudly enough for Zac to hear.

Hillary left the room, and ran down the stairs in tears past Zac and into her safe haven.

Zac stood there looking at the floor covered in red paint.

CHAPTER TEN
A NOT SO SILLY
SUGGESTION

'Will, what have you done with those not so precious gems? Over.'

'I've found a small compartment like a glove box on my lavalorry so I put them in there. Over.'

'I wonder if any nicbeing saw us leave. Over.'

'It was such a rush to get out I didn't think to look back.'

There was a pause.

'Sorry. Over.'

'Let's cut the over shall we?' said Pat.

'Got it, Pat. Where do you think we should go now?'

'Even though we have the not so precious gems I am not sure we are any closer to finding Amy. I really am missing her. I hope she is okay.'

'If I know Amy, and I think I do, she is able to take care of herself.'

'If I'm right and it is Zac who has taken her, she won't stand for any of his nonsense; in fact she'd probably teach him a thing or two.'

'Pull up where you are. I want to take a look back at the twin Hot Spots now we are far enough away.'

'Roger that.'

The lorries pulled up off the track side by side.

'From here, the outside shell looks to be unharmed.'

'We kind of knew that Pat. The damage was caused inside. But look at the outbreak of nicbeings and the state they're in. Most them are covered in sand and debris from the collapse inside.'

'It's so sad to think Pete and Peg have spent their whole lives building the twin Hot Spots and now it's been destroyed.'

'Where do you think we should go from here?'

'What are the choices?'

'Well, the twin Slava Slopes we will pass on our way back, or otherwise we can return to Hugh and Reece.'

'I think we should go and see if they need a hand,' said Pat.

'Back in the lorries we go.'

They travelled along in silence with Will's big lorry mounting over large boulders, down and through what were once river beds, over hills and up sides of volcanos. Pat's light lorry just bounced along behind.

'Pat.'

'What's up?'

'Don't you find it ironic that the one extra thing Amy brings along with her, her ring of calmness as she so fondly refers to it, happens to be exactly our mission here?'

'It is ironic but generally these things happen for a reason.'

'All I did was gave her a hard time about it.'

'She doesn't care, Will; that's what friends do, they have a joke and move on.'

'Speaking of best friends or should I say friendnics, is that Jack in the distance over there?'

Pat used his super seeing. 'I think you're right. How could you see that far and know it was him?'

'I saw this nicbeing moving around and took a guess it was Jack.'

'I wonder what he's doing.'

'Let's pull over and look.'

Will and Pat pulled over and went to watch as Jack was on the front with three other nicbeings in single file behind him. They were straddled on what looked like a solid lava pipe with two smaller pipes, one on each side for them, to put their feet on. They were sliding down the very bottom of one of the twin Slava Slopes. Just prior to when the slope flattened out Jack steered them off course and they all toppled off on top of each other rolling and laughing.

'Ouch, that would have hurt.'

'They don't look to be hurt Will, they're too busy laughing.'

'I know, but the surface they fell to looks like almost dried up solid lava.'

In all the commotion Jack noticed Will and Pat not far in front of him so left the others and walked to them.

'Jack, what's going on?'

Jack looked at them both strangely. He especially stared at Pat. 'Oh, I know where I've seen you before, you were our valls in our vennis game.'

'That's right. I'm Will and this is Pat. He's an animal known as a dog and we both come from planet Earth.'

Jack held his index finger up at Will. 'How did you know I was going to ask what Pat was?'

'I'm clever,' was all Will answered.

If only Jack knew how many times we have had to explain what Pat is, Will thought.

'What have you been doing?' he asked as he lifted his chin in the direction Jack had come from.

Jack looked back at his friendnics. 'Oh they were passing by so we thought we'd take a quick ride on the Slava Sleigh before the lava fully dries.'

'I was wondering why you didn't hurt yourselves when you came off.'

'When the lava is at the temperature it's at now on this level of the mountain it's mushy so you get dirty but coming off doesn't hurt.'

Jack's friendnics walked off as they bade him farewell so he turned and waved back. He looked back at Will and Pat then at the sleigh then back at Will and Pat. 'Do you want to come and have a go?'

Will jumped at the opportunity. 'Yeah, that would be awesome.'

Jack looked at Pat who looked at Will. 'Will, we've a lot to do.'

'Come on Pat, this is a one off chance and the Slava Sleigh looks excellent.'

'How about this; you and Jack go for a ride, I'll head back to meet the others and you can meet me there.'

'You're not going to ride with us?'

'No and you have just one ride down.'

Jack piped up, 'You don't need to worry. We can only slide from just up there where the lava flow stops and the only way up is walking.'

'I don't care, I'm excited,' said Will.

Jack ran to where the sleigh had been abandoned, closely followed by Will. Pat shook his head, remembering that Will was a boy and this was a thrill.

'This sleigh is heavy,' discovered Will.

'Yeah I know, it's because the three pipes that make it up are solid. Put it on your shoulder to carry it up.'

'How did you make it?'

'I didn't. Over on the other Slava Slope the twin to this one there is a Slava Scrap heap. Maanic tells all the nicbeings that work here to put them there.'

'What do you use these pipes for anyway?'

'Nothing at the moment Will. They get thrown away. They are formed dependent on which way the lava flows down the side of the volcanos and the shape of the land in the pathway of that lava. Lately lots of pipes have been formed and they all go to the scrap heap. It's funny because a lot of them are the same length but we've no use for them.'

Will shrugged with no further thought on the topic. He was keen to get the sleigh up the slight slope, but it turned out to be hard work.

'The ride doesn't take long but it's worth it, you'll see,' said Jack.

They got up as far as they could go and put the sleigh down. Jack took the front position. 'Hop on Will, straddle your legs over and hold onto me.'

'You're not going to get me off are you?'

'Maybe,' was all that was said and they took off.

They traversed from side to side as the wind took their hair and blew it backwards. Closer to the bottom in about the same position as last time Jack did his usual party trick and took a sharp right turn, spilling them over. Squeals of joy were heard, so much so they were unable to speak from laughing too much.

'That was the best Will, I managed to get you off quicker than the last go.'

Will laughed at Jack. 'It was awesome. Thanks so much... you're the best, but I better get going.'

'Where have you got to be?'

'Over in the Wasteland.'

Will explained to Jack about Amy's vanishing and his deal to rebuild the Date Wall.

'Why don't I come and help you.'

'What about your work here?'

'Oh Maanic and I just had a fight. That's why I'm here playing. Gees she gives me the poops sometimes.'

Will laughed. 'It doesn't matter where you go or who you meet. Everyone's maanic annoys them sometimes.'

'My maanic Molly excels at it.'

Will belly-laughed. 'That is so funny.'

'It may be funny but it's true. She takes annoying to a whole new level.'

'I think I've got the picture; you and your maanic are not getting on so well right now.'

'Wow Will, what took you so long?'

'Okay, come and help us. An extra set of hands can't hurt.'

'Give me a hand to put the sleigh over near the slava scraps.'

Together Will and Jack put the sleigh away.

'Won't Molly worry about where you are?'

'Naa she'll be fine. She'll be too busy with the Mosaic Moveator and telling the nicbeings how to do their jobs.'

'I want to find out about and ride on the Mosaic Moveator.'

'Later Will, I'll show you later.' Jack followed Will. 'Have you got a lavalorry?'

'Yep, just over here.'

'Aren't they the best! If you don't like the shape you can so easily change it. How good is that?'

'One of my favourite things on Venus apart from vennis and the slava sleigh of course is the lavalorries. I love driving them around.'

'This one is so big you can drive over anything.'

'I know. I chose the shape myself. I always wanted a big tanker.'

'It is true, size does matter.'

Will and Jack both thought that last comment was hysterical.

'You're cool Jack.'

'Thanks Will, but you should meet my friendnic Max.'

'I have. Before we saw you we were at the twin Hot Spots with him Pete and Peg.'

'Speaking of cool, aren't they?'

'They seem easy going.'

'Believe me they are cool.'

'Jack, you do know the twin Hot Spots just got bombarded with burning lava rocks...'

'What?'

'Seriously, not that long ago.'

'Is Max okay?'

'He and Pete were in the lava lator with us so we all got to the surface.'

'Phew, then what happened?'

'Pat and I saw there was panic everywhere so we left.'

'You didn't hang around to help?'

'There was not much we could do plus Pete had a really good evacuation plan for the nicbeings that work there.'

'That is true, Pete has all that stuff covered.'

'Now the sinkhole is in the middle of town it's so much harder to get around.'

'I've been thinking for ages wouldn't it be great if we had an overpass that went from the Lava Hi House to the twin Slava Slopes, over to the twin Hot Spots and most importantly to the Wasteland where my favourite vennis vacket is. There definitely needs to be access there even if it is for self-serving purposes.'

Will laughed at Jack. 'Then I guess you'd also want to build a vennis vadium as well so that when all those spectators that never come finally do, they'll have somewhere to sit. On Earth we call it a stadium but here it would be called a vadium.'' Will was in stitches. He couldn't get over what he'd suggested but Jack looked serious.

'Will, that is genius. That is the best idea ever; a vennis vadium. If you can assemble the Date Wall then you'll sure know how to build a vadium. In fact you can make the new Date Wall part of the vadium.'

Will promptly stopped laughing. The image of Amy's ring with the rays of light flooded his head, and he said, 'Jack, hold on.'

Will floored the lavalorry, leaving a path of sand and dust in his wake. He needed to get back to the others so drove in silence. Poor Jack held on for dear life, having no idea why Will's mood had changed.

Will skidded his lorry so close to where Pat, Hugh and Reece were standing he almost knocked them over and rather than use the rope to lower himself out of his lorry he simply jumped over the side.

All three watched Will, barely noticing Jack who shakily came down from the lorry. Jack walked to the front of the lorry holding onto it.

'We skimmed the track to get here.'

Pat had a smirk. 'Will does have a tendency to put his foot down if he is on a mission.'

Jack looked at Hugh and Reece. 'Hi, I'm Jack,' he announced as he waved with one hand and continued using the lorry for support with the other hand.

Reece responded, 'Hi Jack, I'm Reece and this is Hugh.'

Jack looked at them in astonishment.

'We get it; you've not seen anything that looks like us before.'

Jack nodded. 'You are really good at this, so you must have been asked many times before.'

'Like everywhere we go. I am an ironkidcaptron because I'm made of iron and my sistron (which for you is sisnic here) Reece is a rockkidgemtron. She is made of rock and we come from planet Mercury.'

This time Jack really did look peculiarly at them. 'You're a long way from home.'

'We know that,' responded Hugh proudly.

Will was champing at the bit. 'Pat, Pat.'

'What is it Will?'

'I'm a genius.'

'Yes, go on,' Pat responded suspiciously.

'Jack and I were talking on our way here and he suggested an overpass that joins the Lava Hi House to the twin Hot Spots to the twin Slava Slopes and to the Wasteland. Then I jokingly suggested we build a vennis stadium which up here would be called a vadium where all the spectators could sit when they come to watch Jack and Max play vennis.'

Hugh and Reece broke out laughing with that suggestion but Pat held a straight face.

'See Pat, my reaction was the same as theirs,' he said as he pointed to Hugh and Reece, 'until I remembered the rays of light that Amy's ring showed us.'

Hugh and Reece instantly piped down.

'Once again I had the same reaction as them.'

Pat looked at Will. 'You could be onto something here.'

Will patted his pocket and he felt the ring was still in there. 'I've an idea, just to be sure. I will go back to the sinkhole where we held the ring up and see if the same rays of light appear again. If the ray of light toward the Wasteland does not appear then that will be the site we will build the Date Wall and maybe the stadium.'

'Wait up Will; that all sounds great but they are enormous structures.'

'That's where I can help,' put in Jack. 'I know enough nicbeings on this planet and more than likely know where to get all you will need to build.'

'But what about if what just happened at the twin Hot Spots happens to us while we build?'

'What happened over there Pat?'

'I just told you, remember? Fire burning lava rocks were hurled in and the operation caved in literally.'

'There is no guarantee that won't happen. However, a majority of the nicbeings that were working there will go and work for Henry because they are scared of him. The ones that aren't scared I will ask to help us.'

'Be serious. They are Pete's workers so you can't just go and take them.'

'Leave that to me. I know what to do. After all his sonnic Max is my best friendnic so I might be able to cut a deal.'

'Now I am worried.'

'It's cool Pat, I've got this.'

'Okay team here is where we go from here. Jack, you will need to work out a way to get a ride across to the twin Hot Spots or otherwise go up on your vennis vacket and contact Max to come and get you.'

'Why would I do that when I have my own hand held two way radio here that has an exclusive frequency direct to Max?'

Jack displayed the two way and got through to Max, then walked away to have his conversation.

117

'Will, you adjust my lavalorry from a single seater and take Reece back to the sinkhole and test the ring together,' directed Pat. 'For something like that two heads are better than one.'

Hugh was left standing there with his index finger in the air.

'Don't worry Hugh, I've not forgotten. You will adjust Will's lorry to have a tray at the back then load the left over rocks onto it. From there you will drive Amy's and I will drive Will's to the new home of the Date Wall. Before we unload one single lava rock we will wait for Will and Reece to come back and confirm the ring shows no ray from that side of this planet. Is everything clear?'

Jack walked back to the group in time to hear Pat's question.

'Yes,' they responded in unison.

'One more thing. This is a delicate operation. I need you all so please, please, please be safe.'

'Sure Pat, and thank you,' responded Will as he went over and patted him. 'I should probably change my saying to when there's a Pat there's a way but it doesn't work as well as using my name,' announced Will proudly.

Pat rolled his eyes, 'let's get on with it shall we?'

CHAPTER ELEVEN
STIR UP THE
SINKHOLE

Amy had been scraping gems out of the ceiling for what felt like hours. Every so often when she would tire so she chose between eating a ven-la-roc or lying on the ground to further inspect the ceiling. She knew her ven-la-rocs were limited as she was down to her last two so the lie down was the best option. She thought it was strange that Zac had not been back to check on her. Maybe the exit must be so well hidden even he had trouble finding it to re-enter.

The thought of Zac made her realise she needed to devise a plan to hide her newfound gems for fear he would take them from her.

Eleven little darlings and aren't they beautiful, she thought as she sat cross legged and inspected them one at a time, shining the light on them. *I wonder why eleven. What does that number signify?* Amy tried to work it out as it seemed such an odd number. Now, where to hide them?

The only place she could think they would be safe was in her pockets, as she had nothing more on her. She pulled her last two ven-la-rocs out of her pockets and put five gems in one side and six in the other and the two left of ven-la-rocs on top. She then rose to her feet to see if the weight of them was too much. She walked around and knew it was too much for her pockets but figured it was her only option.

'What if he sees them?' she questioned herself

'Of course he'll see them,' she answered herself. Amy realised she was talking to herself and was conscious it was the first sign of madness but then comforted herself, knowing she was the only one here.

She lay back on the cool ground and pointed the light to the ceiling in search of more gems.

She did not see any sparkles but this time she saw a small drop of liquid. She hoped it might be water so grabbed her stool and climbed up for a closer inspection. She put her finger in it, then inspected it closely before sniffing it. She came to no conclusions.

She stood there longer and another drop formed. This time she saw it was a dull grey colour and this drop was warmer.

'It could be boiling lava!' she exclaimed out loud.

Not knowing what to do about it Amy sat back down on the ground and continued to monitor it in case the flow of drops increased. She got back up to the drops again and put the light up close to see if there would be any change if she melted the area around it. She watched and waited but the droplets formed in their own good time.

She had the two ven-la-rocs but she couldn't work out how they could help. She was aware she had the gems because they were weighing her down but apart from that she felt she had run out of options until she remembered the small bottle of CHAMPET around her neck.

Bravo Amy.

She got the CHAMPET, snapped open the lid and pushed the sides a few times to see what would happen. She questioned herself on what exactly she was trying to achieve but couldn't come up with any definite answer.

After all she had no idea where she was but it was worth a try.

If liquid could get in then maybe there was a way out.

The flow of drops began to increase so Amy kept pumping, hoping a smoke signal was getting out in the atmosphere somewhere.

Will and Reece were half way on their journey to the sinkhole.

'Will, you must be somewhat proud of yourself. So far you've directed us to find the pile of perfectly shaped rocks which we hope will be enough for the Date Wall, then the suggestion of the vadium.'

'I don't know. It's kind of hard when the life of your best friend is riding on it.'

'But if it goes your way and you pull it off, you'll have really kicked a goal.'

'Maybe.'

Will was not usually humble but his mind was on other things. After all doing two things at once was not his forte.

'Reece, did you count all the rocks to make sure there was enough there?' he asked.

'Hugh was handling that. I counted the humps that sit on the top and there were thirteen of them. My gut instinct is they are all there.'

'Good; if you're right, that is one thing that has gone our way. Normally we miss a piece or two here or there.'

'Look around. It's bedlam. The nicbeings are going in all directions.'

'Their planet is deteriorating one structure at a time, remember. It's devastating and there is no infrastructure to back it up.'

'Pretty bad.'

'It is. Now hold on; we're almost there.'

Reece held on as Will put his foot down to get them there sooner. As the crowds had dispersed, Will was able to park more easily.

'We'll park back here where the land is safe and not likely to cave in then walk in as close as we can to the edge.'

'Sounds like a plan Will.'

'I have to warn you, the land surrounding a sinkhole can cave in at any time so tread carefully.'

'Thanks for the tip.' Reece followed Will as he gently took steps and managed to be almost at the edge of the sinkhole.

'Now, where's that ring?' He patted his pockets.

Reece noticed something coming out of the sinkhole. 'Will, can you see that? It looks like a puff of smoke coming off those air bubbles.'

Will briefly looked. 'Reece, it's boiling lava, so smoke will definitely be coming off it.'

She was not convinced so she kept her eyes hard on the spot that had caught her attention in the first place.

Meanwhile, Will was still fussing about looking for the ring. He put his hand into his pocket and pulled out his magnifier and with it came his ven-la-roc. He went to catch it but it hit the back of one of his fingers and flung into the sinkhole.

'Oh no!'

A geyser erupted instantaneously, forcing Will and Reece to step back to avoid getting wet. It lasted only seconds but they both stood there gobsmacked.

'What was that?' asked Reece.

'It was my one and only ven-la-roc, the one I got on the way here.'

'Did you see what happened?' Whether it was the ven-la-roc or the boiling lava in the sinkhole, it unleashed a geyser.'

Will was lost for words so he bent down and put his finger on the part of the ground that was moist from the geyser.

'Did that geyser let out boiling lava or water?'

'That's what I'm checking Reece but it looks like water to me. There is a small crevice here; I'll taste it.'

Reece stood, trying to be patient. 'And?'

'It's definitely water.'

'Yeah, we've found water on Venus!' she screamed with joy.

Will on the other hand was disappointed. 'That was my one and only ven-la-roc and the only way we can get more is from Hillary.'

Reece stood smiling. 'It may have been your only one but I have plenty.' She pulled out two big handsful of them and was about to throw them in the sinkhole.

'Wait up Reece!' Will caught her wrist, then bent again to get closer to the sinkhole. 'Ven-la-rocs are scarce and we'll need them.' He held his magnifier up and pointed it toward the direction Reece had previously seen the unusual smoke.

'What are you looking at?' she asked as she put the ven-la-rocs away.

'You might be onto something about that puff of smoke over there. I thought I'd take a look and see if my magnifier can shed anything. Bend down here and have a look.'

'There's an unusual puff of smoke and through the magnifier the smoke is showing as pink,' she said.

They were silent for second while they watched what happened.

'The smoke keeps puffing out, but it's coming out thicker and faster.'

'But watch, it looks like two small letters are there, but I'm not sure what they are.'

'Will,' shrieked Reece as she grabbed his arm. 'It's Amy. The smoke is pink and it's formed the letters H and I for hi. On Mercury before Maatron left for the rock village she told me of the deal she had made with Amy that if you needed help finding Hugh, to look up in the sky at the smoke. Those CHAMPET bottles around your neck... if you puff them...'

'Yes, yes I know,' he said as he stopped her. 'But on Mercury HR was help Rocktrons and it came up in pink smoke. HI was help Irontrons and that was blue smoke. Here it's HI but in pink smoke.'

'Will, it's Amy anyway. She is stuck under here. It's a different planet a different time HI just means Hi. She is trying to say hello to us.'

'OMG Reece, imagine if you're right.' Will could not contain his excitement. 'What are we going to do, how are we going to get her out of a boiling pond of lava known as a sinkhole? We can't dive in.'

They both squatted on the side watching the smoke through the magnifier as the letters HI became clearer and clearer. Reece scratched the top of her rock leg and brushed her finger over the ven-la-rocs.

'Ven-la-rocs. It's a risk nothing at all may happen and we may not get any more but Amy is worth the risk.'

Will was sweating, and he started pacing.

'We have to get this right as we only get one shot.'

Reece was much calmer. 'What's to get right? You take half, I'll have the other half and on the count of three we throw them in the same area and see what happens. What other option is there?'

Will swallowed. 'I just hope it works and that she's okay.'

Reece pulled out all the ven-la-rocs she had.

'By the way how did you get so many of these?' asked Will.

'It pays to hang with Amy. She offered to help Hillary and when Hillary's back was turned and some of the ven-la-rocs fell on the ground I snatched up as many as I could.'

'Did Amy get any?'

'She sure did but not as many as me. She was preoccupied talking with Hillary. Come on Will, we're delaying the inevitable.'

'On the count of three! Ready? One, two... three.'

Together they tossed all the ven-la-rocs they had into the sinkhole on the spot the smoke was coming from. The reaction was as if the sinkhole divided down the middle to make an entrance for an outstanding unleashed geyser. The geyser let out its first shot as though warming up then it spouted again except this time up through the middle of it came Amy! She rode up on the geyser and was at the top of it like the queen of the world. Will was shell shocked.

'Amy, over here!' Reece screamed, hoping Amy would turn her head and she did as she screamed back. 'Catch me Will!'

Amy jumped from the top of the geyser soaking wet and was caught by both Reece and Will as they had joined their hands together to make a cradle. She stood up and gave Will a big hug.

'Thank goodness, you saved me.'

She then turned to Reece and gave her the same big hug.

'Amy, you're safe!'

'I don't know how you found me but I'm sure glad you did. It was boring and lonely in that dark place all alone.'

'Where were you?'

'I don't really know but it was a hot dark room and I had no idea how to get in or get out of there.'

'But how did you get there in the first place?' asked Will. 'You just vanished.'

'You're not going to believe it. There is another human here on Venus with us and you'll never guess who it is!'

'I have an idea,' said Will. 'Does his name start with Z?'

'How did you know?'

'I didn't. I guessed.'

'Are you two talking about the Zac human that used to be your best friend? The one you made the pact with?'

'Yep,' said Will.

'How did he get here then?'

'I have no idea how he got here but he is in cahoots with Henry.'

'Lava Hi House Henry?'

'Yep. They are planning to blast the twin Hot Spots and the twin Slava Slopes. We'd better hurry...' Her words died away as she saw the look Will exchanged with Reece. 'What?'

'You're a tad late on the warning for the twin Hot Spots,' said Will. 'They have destroyed them.'

'What about the twin Slava Slopes?'

'At this moment they're fine.'

'Um, look at the sinkhole,' said Reece.

Will and Amy turned to see the geyser was reduced to a small bubble of water boiling up from the surface until it finally stopped. The water had hardened the lava leaving the outside circumference of the sinkhole with a solid mound of lava in the middle of it.

'Whoops, was that meant to happen?'

'I don't know Ames.'

'The main thing is that we got Amy back safely. Whether the sinkhole was meant to solidify is another thing.'

Will bent and rubbed his hand on it.

'I'm excited Amy is here but Venus needs water and I thought we'd found a way of getting it.'

Amy stared at the ground. 'Will, the stuffy dark room I was in was cool on the floor but boiling hot on the roof. What was here before?'

'The Date Wall.'

'That's right, we were on our way to the Date Wall when Hugh and I broke down and Zac swooped past, put a bag over my head and took me. It happened so fast, I had no idea.'

'Poor Hugh was feeling so bad about losing you on his watch,' said Reece.

'And to add salt to the wound I was harsh on him about it.'

'Ease up on him Will, it could have happened just the same if you and I were together.'

Will nodded.

'Anyway, as I was saying the floor was cool which only makes me think there is water under this sinkhole but something is stopping it from exploding out.'

'We threw ven-la-rocs in that seem to have broken through the boiling lava and freed the water.'

'That's brilliant Reece. How did you work that out?'

'Purely by accident. Will dropped his in and a small geyser exploded. Then I had plenty from the ones I picked up from the floor when we were with Hillary so we threw them all at once and thus it freed you.'

'Wow, those ven-la-rocs are really something.'

Reece looked at Amy's bulging pockets. 'You look to have stacks of them in your pockets.'

Amy's thoughts were elsewhere, and it took her a moment to register what Reece had said. 'I've only two ven-la-rocs left.' She reached into her pocket and pulled them out.

Now Will was looking at her pockets. 'What else have you got in there Ames?'

She pulled out the square shaped amethyst. 'I found a whole load of these stones. I can't believe how beautiful they are so I thought I'd take them home.'

Will grabbed the stone out of Amy's hand. 'Ames, sometimes you are very cute.'

'What are you talking about Will?'

'Yeah, I'd like to know too,' chimed in Reece.

'These not so precious stones as they like to refer to them as are part of the Date Wall. Where two humps meet at the top they are marked with these stones and for the nicbeings that live here it marks the months of the year.'

'They have months on Venus?'

'Not really, but as Venus is Earth's twin they use the same months as us.'

'How do you know that?'

'Marky, the Date Wall master told us. We met him just after you went missing.'

'Gee, I bet I've missed a lot and won't be able to catch up with the nicbeings that you've met.'

'Of course you will,' reassured Reece.

'Ames, I'm guessing you know things that we don't know.'

'Maybe. Nonetheless,' she said as she took the stone back from him, 'I lost my ring so I figured even just one of these stones could replace it.'

Will laughed. 'Sorry to burst your bubble but we will be needing all twelve of your stones for the new Date Wall.'

'Twelve?'

'Yeah, surely you have twelve of them.'

'No I don't, I only have eleven.' She started to pull them out.

'Okay, okay, I believe you.'

Reece elbowed Will and he looked at her in astonishment. 'Don't you have something of Amy's?'

'Of course,' Will said as he fumbled into his pocket. He pulled out Amy's ring.

Her face lit up with excitement as she put it back on her finger. 'Thank you so much. I feel better already having it on my finger.'

'That ring is special. Now we're here by what was the Date Wall, then a sinkhole and now a mound hole, I guess if that makes sense. Hold up your hand.'

As she held it up a ray beamed from it to the Lava Hi House, to the twin Hot Spots to the twin Slava Slopes but nothing toward the Wasteland.

'That's weird.'

'We thought so too when we first discovered it but here's what we've worked out. What do you call that ring?'

'My ring of calmness.'

'Right so we think it is indicating to us the ring of calmness. In order to get calmness there needs to be a structure in the direction of the Wasteland. Reece and I are here for the sole purpose of making sure the ring is still indicating the ring of calmness. Finding you was an added bonus and I'm sure glad you're back,' he mentioned as he put his arm around her shoulder.

'Me too.' She patted his back. 'Where is Pat?'

'He's back at the site where we want to rebuild the Date Wall.'

'Then what are we waiting for?'

Will drove them all back to meet with the others.

CHAPTER TWELVE
AMY'S BACK AND THE
WAR BEGINS

'Pat, Pat, look who we found.'

Pat looked up to see Will screaming at him but had no idea what he was saying so he stood watching until the lavalorry came closer.

'Look who we found Pat.'

Pat and Hugh stood they could not believe what they were seeing.

'Amy,' yelled Hugh as he ran and assisted her out of the lorry and hugged her.

'I'm glad to see you too but please, not so tight. I can hardly breathe.'

He only slightly loosened his grip.

'All right Hugh, I got the message. Let me go!'

Hugh unwillingly let her go and she knelt beside Pat.

'Amy, my darling Amy,' was all that was said as she hugged him.

'How did you two find her?' asked Hugh.

'It's normally Pat who is fond of grand entrances but on this occasion Amy rose out of a geyser.'

Hugh stood looking at Will as though he had four heads. Will sensed Hugh did not understand so he explained everything, including Zac's part in the affair.

Meanwhile, Reece walked off to inspect the rocks they had acquired on the back of the lorries.

'How many there?' asked Will when he'd finished his explanation.

'I think Hugh will be able to confirm but from my calculations we have enough to build the wall.'

Will looked at Hugh, who nodded. 'Reece is right.'

'Super!' commended Will.

'Will, you mentioned assembling the Date Wall but you didn't mention how.'

'I can explain that,' said Hugh. He took Amy by the hand and led her to where all the rocks were stacked in the back of the lorries and explained what they were going to do.

Minutes later Pat cut in. 'All, I'm so excited that my Amy is back and that we have a plan to assemble the wall but there must be a combat plan in the event we get hit or the structure gets hit by burning lava rocks.'

'Agreed Pat, what have you got?'

Pat looked at Will. 'Nothing definite at the moment. We might need Jack and Max for this.'

'Jack and Max, the vennis players are helping us now,' put in Reece.

'How did it happen?'

'Not completely sure but Pat and Will have managed to get them on side.'

'Here they come now,' said Amy.

'Will, Will,' Max yelled at him as the lorry halted. 'You stole our not so precious gems.'

Will said nothing, his face reddening.

'Will, I know you did.'

Pat stepped in. 'Max, calm down. We do have them and intend to borrow them. We promise once our project is complete we'll return them if possible.'

'But what am I going to tell Paanic?'

'The same as I said to you. Tell him that Will and Pat are temporarily borrowing them.'

Will finally found his tongue. 'Max, since your famnic's mining operation has temporarily ceased I am sure you won't be needing them.'

'Probably not, but at least you could have asked.'

'There was no time,' said Will. 'Besides, we both know if we'd have asked there is no way Pete would have let us.'

'Probably not but at least I know where they are.'

'Now that is sorted,' said Pat, 'we really need your help.'

'Don't worry. There will be nicbeings arriving shortly to help.'

'That's great but there is a new piece to the puzzle.' Pat swung his head in Amy's direction.

Jack scrunched up one side of his nose so Pat more definitely swung his head.

Amy caught onto what he was trying to do. 'Jack and Max, I am Amy. Pat is trying to make you aware that I'm now here.'

'Hi Amy nice to meet you, but I still don't understand.'

'My darling dog is not normally short of words so on this occasion I'll help. Will and Reece have set me free from the clutches of Henry's helper, Zac. He is another human like us. Pat is worried, now I've escaped, that Zac will come after us harder and faster especially if we start to build the Date Wall.'

'How did you work all that out?'

'Quite easy, Pat. You know I've been gone for a while and all I had was time to think. Will told me you were rebuilding and now I've met Zac. I have no idea how he and Will could ever be friends and I know he's capable of retaliating, especially now I'm free.'

'I'm very impressed,' said Pat.

'You should be. I feel proud when you are proud.'

'So back to my original request. How can we use the vennis vackets and some of the boulders in the wasteland to break the burning lava rocks if they are hurled at us or at the under-construction Date Wall?'

Jack and Max grinned.

'We have the answer,' responded Max.

'Okay, just do what's needed when the time comes.'

'Deal,' said Max.

By this stage Will had used the magnifier to find the right spot and scratched into the ground where the wall would stand. Like the perfect team the others started to unload the rocks, placing them one beside the other in the allocated areas. Pat, Jack and Max all went to look on as Will stood up.

'The only piece of the puzzle I can't work out is how we are going to bind the rocks together,' said Will.

Jack smirked. 'With the running lava from the twin Slava Slopes of course.'

'Of course,' Will repeated.

By the time Will had turned, Jack and Max had gathered around him and tumbled him over like a play wrestle. They both hastily got up. Jack took off in Pat's lorry and Max took off in his own.

'Let's hope they'll return with the lava.'

When they were a fair enough distance away. Jack fired up the two way. 'Did you get it?'

'Sure did, Jack. The magnifier's now mine.'

'An eye for an eye, Max.'

'Absolutely. They took our not so precious gems, so it's only fair I've got his magnifier.'

'Be careful with it Max. We all know how powerful it is.'

'Don't worry, I just want to have some fun. I know I have to give it back but I'll do so when he gives the gems back. Paanic will be proud.'

'At least you've got something to bargain over with Henry.'

'Yeah Jack, exactly. Where are you going now?'

'I did promise to get some lava to help build the wall. Thought I'd head off and do that.'

'I'll give the magnifier a go then I'll have to go and tell Paanic.'

'Are you sure you'll be okay?'

'What could possibly happen? Apart from you no nicbeing knows I've got it.'

'Okay. See you back there when you've sorted it with your paanic.'

'Bye Jack. Over.'

'Over and out Max.'

Max detoured over toward the sinkhole and noticed a large mound of lava was now where a hole once was.

'Wow this has changed. I wonder what happened?' he murmured to himself as he pulled his lorry up. He grabbed the magnifier and went to stand at the edge. He held the magnifier up and beamed through it, marvelling at all magnified shapes and textures of the lava mound. The part he was most obsessed with was the amazing colour changes in the lava.

Max was having such a great time he decided he needed to study the mound from all sides so took his time and did exactly that.

The red paint on the floor was reflected in Zac's face after overhearing Henry and Hillary's argument. Zac decided it was time to take matters in his own hands so promptly escaped from the Hi House in his lavalorry and headed back to his secret room. On the way however he ground to a halt as he saw Will in the distance with a group around him constructing something.

What is he doing? Zac thought as he watched on from afar.

He admitted to himself that he'd always admired Will but was not able to get over the immeasurable envy he had for him. The envy began the day Will saved Zac from the school bullies. Realistically Zac should have been grateful but the feelings went the other way and Zac went home that night and fed his mother so much false information about Will that it caused her to react against their friendship.

Even though Zac realised his nasty streak he was still determined to stop Will on whatever quest he was to undertake. He'd seen enough now so he turned. On his way past the sinkhole he swerved around a nicbeing crouched down looking through something. Zac hurried by half looking back and noticing a reflection from the instrument the nicbeing held.

Intrigued, he u-turned back and parked his lorry beside the other one that was there. He crept up on the nicbeing, peered over his shoulder and realised he was holding the precious magnifier.

He drew a deep breath to calm himself. 'Hmmmm, what are you doing there?'

Max gasped and turned. 'Hi. You scared me.'

Zac could not take his eyes off the prize. This was it; his big moment had arrived and the magnifier was in his sight.

'It looks like fun,' he said casually. 'What were you looking at?'

'I was studying the formation of the lava. It's interesting how it forms in layers.'

Zac had no interest in that. 'Hmmmm.'

Max turned and continued his examination.

Zac realised he needed to make more of an effort. 'Well...why don't I look with you?'

'Can if you want,' was all Max replied.

Zac crouched there for a while and then Max piped up. 'You're not from here.'

'Is it that obvious?'

'Yes,' was all Max was willing to say.

This conversation was hard work.

'I am a human from planet Earth.'

'I know.'

'How do you know that?'

'I've met others like you. I even know what dogs are.'

Zac gathered Max must have met his nemesis Will otherwise he wouldn't have the magnifier. He asked, 'Where did you get that thing you have in your hand? What's it called?'

'Magnifier.'

'Did someone give it to you?'

'Maybe.'

'Gee dude, don't give me too much info.'

'I didn't ask you to hang.'

'No but I am, because I want it.'

Zac lunged over Max and grabbed the magnifier from his grip. Max was quick to fight back and punched Zac in the stomach. Zac was temporarily winded but as Max went to reach for the magnifier back Zac kicked Max with enough force to push him backwards. Zac, always better as a coward than a fighter, scrambled to his feet and bolted to his lorry to take off at breakneck speed directly back to the Lava Hi House.

Max felt the brunt of the kick to the stomach so was face down until he caught his breath. He put his hand on his cheek and felt a deep scratch in his lava face.

Zac swooped into the garage door that he'd left opened and slammed it shut, making sure there was no one behind him. He put the magnifier in his back pocket and made his way to the platform where the red paint had now dried and Henry was surveying the scene.

Henry heard the garage door slam and turned. 'What happened here you useless—'

Zac was scared but decided to act cool as after all it seemed to work for Amy. 'Cool your jets dude!'

Henry had never heard such a thing so was unable to make comment.

'So, I spilt a little red paint, and I went to the garage to see if there was anything to clean it up. Now I'm going to ask Hillary.'

Zac bent to open the trapdoor and Henry noticed an instrument in his back pocket.

'No you don't,' screamed Henry as he stomped his foot on the door and slammed it out of Zac's clutch. 'You're not going down there. You've only put one line of the cross on the door, you've been out without telling me and it seems you've brought something back.'

Zac was shaking; his cool demeanour gone. 'I was going to clean it up.'

'I'm more interested in what you've bought back,' stated Henry pointing his finger to end of Zac's nose.

'Well I...'

'Well you what? What have you got?' yelped Henry.

Zac carefully reached into his back pocket where he could feel immense heat radiating from the magnifier. It was so hot he could barely hand it to Henry.

Henry's eyes widened. 'Where did you get this?'

'I found it by the sinkhole.'

Henry put his face right up to Zac's. 'Do you think I'm really going to believe you?'

Zac was a nervous wreck, as beads of sweat dripped down his face. He was willing to say anything to get Henry off him. 'Henry, I saw this aquanic with it and I rolled him for it. Take it; it's yours.' The magnifier was burning Zac's hand so he gave it willingly to Henry who was scalded when he touched it. He couldn't handle it so the magnifier flew up in the air and in seeming slow motion came down and hit the ground. It bounced and Henry took a step back just as the magnifier wedged its way under Henry's heel and crunched.

Henry looked at Zac who was looking at Henry then they both looked at the ground to survey the damage.

During the upheaval Hillary had arrived through the trapdoor and happened to be standing there when Henry's heel cracked the magnifier.

'Well done Henry, you sure are putting your foot in everything,' she said.

She turned on her heel and went back downstairs.

Henry bent to pick up the cooled down magnifier. It now had a large crack on the screen and a shard of the glass left behind on the floor.

'What do we do now?' asked Zac.

Henry shrugged. 'I don't care about the crack. While I have this magnifier and the Indicator then I can still control and rule Venus.'

Zac thought he should delight in Henry's good fortune, so he started laughing somewhat hysterically along with Henry. 'You're the best Henry. How could a stupid magnifier outsmart you.'

'That's right Zaccy. I'm the ruler on Venus. Look at my doors, two structures down and one to go... The nicbeings will have to do what I say.'

'They're assembling a new Date Wall,' Zac blurted out.

Henry looked sternly at Zac. 'Where?'

'Over by the Wasteland.'

'And who is *they*?' Henry's momentary happy mood had once again clicked to anger mode.

'Those humans that are here.'

Henry frowned. 'How would they be able to do that?'

'I don't know sir, but I saw them, and they looked to have everything they need. There were even some nicbeings heading over there.'

'It's not possible; all the nicbeings from the twin Hot Spots should be on their way here. I am the only one who has work for them.'

'Maybe not!'

Henry looked at Zac with evil in his eyes. 'We must stop them.'

'Henry,' said a voice behind him.

'Not now Hillary. I have much bigger things to worry about.'

'Okay. Our army is not coping with the pellets and shovels that are being hurled at the Hi House. I don't care if you don't care.'

Henry's interest was piqued

'Look out your front door Henry. We are being surrounded.'

Henry still wanted to do things his way. 'This is war,' he declared. He grabbed Zac by the ear and took him to a room where he had an endless supply of lava rocks. He turned on the machine that filled and lit the rocks then opened the door to set the first one free. It hit the ground and bowled the nicbeings that were in its path surrounding the Lava Hi House out of the way, killing some and injuring others

'That took care of some. Now you take over while I go up and have a look at this new Date Wall.'

Zac took an easier approach. He set the next one off making sure it was a scare tactic rather than aimed at annihilation.

Henry ran as fast as his old legs would take him to the top and looked through his mega fixed-to-the-floor binoculars directly at the Wasteland. Sure enough a structure was going up.

'Damn them!' he stormed.

Realising he was buckling under the pressure and that he couldn't call Hillary for assistance or to ask her how to fix the situation, he worked himself up even more by running around in circles trying to work out what to do. He peered through the magnifier that was still in his hand but the crack and lost shard of glass made it impossible to use so he shoved it in his pocket.

I'll set burning lava rocks on them and break that structure down, he decided. Henry's brain did not work as well as it used to so remembering where all his supplies were and how they worked was a challenge in itself. He paced a bit longer until finally he remembered he had a secret stash of rocks up here in case he needed them. He went into his hideaway area and struggled to find the light. He went over to the machine that had never been used and attempted to switch it on. It did not respond. Henry sat down in a huff with sweat pouring from all his pores.

'What are we going to do now, Pete?' asked Peg.

'I'm relieved all the nicbeings are safe,' said Pete. 'We didn't lose any in the avalanche.'

'That's thanks to your smart thinking and tireless effort to have all safety procedures in place.'

'Thanks, but I can't take all the praise; the nicbeings that work for us are the ones that followed the instructions to a tee.' Pete sighed. 'I'd really like to know who took the not so precious gems.'

'That is a mystery. Let's hope they'll turn up.'

'Paanic, Maanic.'

Pete and Peg turned at the sound of Max's voice.

'Paanic, Maanic.'

They watched as he wove his lavalorry through the crowd of nicbeings pushing to exit in the opposite direction.

He jumped out and ran towards them, puffing and almost tripping over.

'What happened to you?' asked Peg, referring to the noticeable scratch on his face.

'I got rolled.'

'Who did it?'

'Paanic, don't panic, it's not that bad.'

'Panic? He may not panic, but I will.'

'Maanic please.'

Pete was good in crisis situations. 'Max, now calm down and explain to us exactly what happened.'

Max caught his breath. 'When the burning lava rocks were being pelted at us, I noticed Will and Pat leave via one of the private offices. I went into where they had exited from and noticed the not so precious gems had gone missing. Since they were the last there I figured it was them.'

Pete looked at Peg. 'That might be true.'

'It is, it is, I promise it is.'

'How can you be sure, Max?'

'I told Jack and we went over and asked them.'

'Max, for something like this, you can't tell Jack and take it on yourselves.'

Pete put his hand on Peg's shoulder. 'Wait up love; let's hear what he did. They are young aquanics.'

Peg nodded, agreeing to hear the story out.

'What happened then, Max? What did they say?'

'They admitted to it.'

'Is that all they said?'

Max shook his head. 'They said I should tell you that they temporarily borrowed them.'

'Temporarily borrowed... what does that mean?' asked Pete.

'That's how I felt, Paanic. So I figured an eye for an eye.'

'You were not bought up with that attitude!' snapped Peg.

Once again Pete calmed Peg and waited for the rest of the story. 'What did you do then Max?'

'Jack and I had a play wrestle with Will and I took the magnifier from him. Then I ran off in my lorry and Jack did the same.'

'You both left the scene of the crime?'

'Yep,' replied Max, very proud of himself.

'How did you get the scratch, Max?'

'This part is not so good. I went to what used to be the sinkhole which is now a mound of solid lava.'

This was news to Pete and Peg so once again they looked at each other, shocked.

'And I was so intrigued by the all the shapes and colours I stayed there gazing through the magnifier.'

'Max, get to the point. You still have not explained the scratch.'

'While I was there another human came along. He started talking to me and before I knew he rolled me and took the magnifier from me.'

'And then?'

'I tried to fight him Paanic but he was bigger than me and he had kicked me in the guts. I was winded so he got away.'

'Are you feeling okay?'

'Yes Maanic, I am fine.'

'Max, the gems are not precious and you already know that. Are you sure this was all worth it?'

'Probably not Paanic but I would not have known if I didn't give it a go.'

'It's what you do at that age dear,' explained Peg to Pete.

'Well the magnifier's gone. There is not much we can do about that but we can get the gems back.'

'No Paanic, Will and Pat assured me they have temporarily borrowed them and I believe them.'

Pete did a fake laugh. 'There is no such thing as borrowing not so precious gems Max. Do you think I just came down in the last lava fall?'

'Paanic, it does sound absurd but I believe them and I think you should too.'

'Why? What proof have you?'

'None really. All I know is they are trying to assemble a new Date Wall and then they are going to build a vennis vadium so finally nicbeings might come and watch Jack and me when we play.'

This time Pete really laughed. 'Max, you're being naïve.'

'No Paanic, I'm not.'

Peg put her hand on Max's shoulder. She saw he really believed in what he was saying. 'Darling, sometimes things are said that are not really meant.'

'But it's true Maanic, I've seen it for myself.'

'You've seen what exactly?'

'The Date Wall. They have started on it over by the Wasteland and the vennis vacket.'

'Oh.'

Pete and Peg looked at each other.

'You want to know another thing Jack told me?'

'Sure Max.'

'They're even going to build an overpass to connect the twin Hot Spots with the Lava Hi House, the twin Slava Slopes and the new Date Wall.'

'Now you're really pulling our legs Max.'

'I'm not, Paanic. If you don't believe me why don't you come and see for yourself? If what I'm telling you is true then you need to load some of your machinery to help.'

Pete rolled his eyes. 'Max, if you believed what you are saying why did you steal Will's magnifier?'

'I couldn't help myself, it's awesome and it's the most sought-after instrument in the universe.'

'But you know what can happen in the wrong hands.'

'I know Paanic and I've learnt my lesson. Now I have the chance to make it up to Will.'

'With my help of course.'

'That's why you are the paanic and I am the childnic.'

'Max if and I mean *if* what you say is true not only will I lend the machinery but I'll get in and help.'

Peg looked at Pete. 'Don't promise him anything you're not going to follow through with.'

'I know what I'm doing.'

Max ran off and Pete turned to follow.

Peg grabbed his arm. 'Darling, if what he says is right and they do intend to connect all the structures on Venus, these twin Hot Spots will be very much sought after.'

'That thought did cross my mind but there is a lot of digging to do to get back to where we were.'

'It can all be done,' she assured him.

Max took his own lorry and Pete and Peg followed as they headed to the Wasteland.

CHAPTER THIRTEEN
THE MAGNIFIER'S
MISSING AGAIN

'What do you think, Ames? Do we position this rock here?'

'I don't know. Look through your magnifier and see what it shows you.'

Will put his hand into his back pocket but nothing was there. Panic roared through him. He reassured himself he had to have it so felt around in his two front pockets. He anxiously felt his back pockets again but nothing.

'The magnifier's missing.'

Amy did not believe it. 'You had it a few seconds ago.'

'I know but...' Will thought back to when Jack and Max had play-wrestled with him. He even recalled feeling it was being removed but had been concentrating so hard on erecting the wall correctly with the aquanic one side and the libnic the other he'd ignored the feeling.

'Jack and Max.'

'What do you mean Will?' asked Pat who had now joined them.

'Either Jack or Max has taken The magnifier.'

'Why would they want the magnifier?' asked Amy.

Will looked at Pat. 'Pat knows why, blame him.'

'You losing the magnifier is your problem not Pat's. Don't blame him,' said Amy.

'Is it? Why don't you ask Pat?'

'What's gotten into you?'

'All I am trying to do is to assemble this damn wall. Firstly Amy goes missing, we almost get blown up in the attack on the twin Hot Spots, we've got to be careful not to get blown up while we're here, and then I get rolled by two... I don't know what you call them.'

'Aquanics will do.'

'Aquanics... and now the magnifier's missing. Let me know when this starts to be fun.'

Will threw his hands in the air and walked off in a huff.

Amy, Pat, Hugh and Reece all stood there staring after him.

'I guess when he puts it like that a lot has happened,' said Pat.

'True, but Will is the one who normally embraces the adventure. There's more to this.'

'You're probably right, Amy. Do you want to talk to him?'

'I'll try.'

Pat, Hugh and Reece all returned to the wall while Amy skipped over to Will. 'Okay, what's eating you?'

Will ran his hand through his hair. 'Ames, it's so great you're back but Zac being here on Venus with us and working with Henry has me really worried.'

'Now I've met him I can't believe you were ever friends. He's not half the person you are.'

'You have to say that; you're my best friend.'

'I may be your best friend but I don't have to say anything. I don't know what his and Henry's plans are but we know what ours are. Let's keep our eyes on what we're doing and get on with it. I like it here and I love the nicbeings but I don't want to stay forever. Let's make this place better than we found it and return to being stars in that show.'

Will and Amy laughed together.

'You always wanted to be a star, didn't you Ames.'

'Not me. It's you that cares for the fame. I'll manage your fortune from your fame.'

They got back to work.

'All sorted?'

'Yes Pat, all sorted. None of this is your fault and I was way out of line. Now what will we do about the magnifier?'

Pat turned to see Jack arriving, followed by an entourage of lavalorries carrying much needed liquid lava. 'There's one of the culprits right there.'

Will made a beeline for Jack while Hugh instructed the rest of the entourage on what to do with the boiling lava.

'Jack, where's my magnifier?'

Jack looked at Will with an absent look. Within a few seconds it registered what Will had just asked. 'Are you talking about the magnifier that is the most sought after instrument in the universe?'

'Uh huh.'

'The same one that all the planets want?'

'Ahhh yeah.'

'The same one Cyril himself would take if he could?'

'That would be it Jack. Stop messing with me, where is it?' Will held out his hand.

'I don't have it,' responded Jack as he skirted around Will.

'I know either you or Max has it,' shouted Will after Jack.

'I don't have it and that's definite.'

'Bloody aquanics,' Will cursed as he walked back to his lorry. 'Hugh, can you get my lorry emptied? I need it.'

Hugh signalled to some of the helping aquanics and libnics to take the last two of the rocks from the back of Will's lorry. 'Where are you going?'

'I'm going to find Max and get my magnifier back.'

'How do you know where to look for him?' asked Amy.

'I'm going to start at the twin Hot Spots then work my way from there.'

'Let me come with you.'

'No, your help is needed here.'

Pat spoke up. 'Amy and I will both come with you.'

Will stared into thin air. 'Okay Pat whatever you think.'

Amy and Pat hopped in with Will and waved to Hugh and Reece. 'We'll be back.'

The trio travelled in silence for the first part of the journey. There was so many thoughts in Will's head he would be surprised if the others could not hear them. He guessed that these, added to the jolting and bouncing around of the terrain they were travelling over, would send anyone's head spinning.

'There's a lorry up ahead and I think you will be most interested in the driver,' said Pat.

'I can't see anything,' said Amy.

'Have faith Amy. My super sight is working.'

'Is the aquanic alone?'

'Maybe.'

'What does maybe mean?'

'It means maybe his paanic and maanic are in the lorry just behind.'

'Gees, nothing is easy.'

'Do me a favour, Will. Hear him out first before you pounce on him.'

'At this moment I can't even see him.'

'He'll come into view shortly.'

Sure enough exactly what Pat had said happened. Max was oncoming so Will stopped his lorry, blocking the thoroughfare, giving Max no choice but to stop. Pete and Peg were right there also.

Will shot out. 'Give me back the magnifier.'

'Hold your horses there Will. We could demand that you give us back our not so precious gems.'
Pete had taken control.

Will rolled his eyes. 'If you want those gems that aren't that precious back so badly then here.'

He went to the secret compartment where he had them hidden. 'Here they are, take them.'

Amy was not exactly sure what was in the sack but she held her hands close to her pockets, hoping hers wouldn't be noticed.

'Will, did you steal those?'

'It's a long story Ames.'

'I'm interested. Why don't you tell it me?' asked Pete.

'Me also,' added Peg.

Pat knew it was time he stepped up. 'I encouraged Will to take these gems. I didn't encourage the behaviour to cause harm or to make enemies but rather because they are a large part of our project and we had no time to ask you.'

'What project is that?' questioned Pete.

'I told you already Paanic, they are assembling a new Date Wall.'

'Max is right. Will made a deal with Marky the Date Wall master to attempt to find and assemble a new Date

Wall in exchange for help finding his best friend Amy whom we have now found.' Pat pointed to Amy who introduced herself and shook hands with Pete, Peg and Max. 'Now we have Amy back, we believe these gems are an integral part to the completion of the wall. We didn't actively go looking for them. It was chance we exited out through one of your secret offices and there they were. Not knowing the future of the twin Hot Spots I figured they would be safe with us and would provide a very important piece to the puzzle.'

'Although the way you went about it was probably not the best, I do understand the motive.'

'Thank you Pete.'

Will still had the sack in his hand and was holding it out to Pete.

'Keep them, Will. Max has explained to me what you are trying to do and if you pull it off we will be very grateful.'

'I won't know unless I try.'

'Peg and I have always thought there has to be another way around Henry, we just never knew how.'

'Hold up there Pete. Assembling a new Date Wall will not guarantee any changes in Henry's behaviour.'

'I know that but it's a start in doing something different. If you want a different result you need to do something different.'

'That's true. Now that we've resolved the matter of the not so precious gems, where is my extremely precious magnifier?'

Max looked down. 'I lost it.'

'You what?'

'I lost it,' Max repeated again in a very soft voice.

'How could you, Max?' Will screeched.

'I was using it at what was the sinkhole and I got rolled by another one like you. A human.'

Will did not comment but rather held his anger and walked off throwing his fists in all directions. Pat and Amy went after him.

'First he takes Amy, now he's taken the magnifier. Who knows? He's so stupid he's probably given it to Henry.'

Pete, Peg and Max walked to where the others were. 'This doesn't sound good.'

Pat, in a clear, calm voice explained the whole situation to Pete, Peg and Max. Pete put his hand on Will's shoulder. 'Will, lead the three of us back to the Date Wall while you Pat and Amy work the best plan you can to get the magnifier back.'

Not a word was spoken as the three lorries arrived.

'Max, take a look, the wall is starting to take shape.'

Max alighted from his lorry and ran to be with Jack. Pete and Peg were impressed.

'How did you find the rocks so perfectly symmetrical Will?'

'It's called trash and treasure. One nicbeing's trash is a human's treasure.'

They all laughed at Will's comment.

Will looked at Pete. 'How do you feel about helping? I mean this is a huge project and your expertise would make things a lot easier.'

'Max tells me you're going to construct an overpass that connects us all. Is that true?'

Will was astonished. 'Why did he tell you that?'

'He said Jack told him.'

'Ahhhh.' Will was not sure how to answer but he thought he just got another clue.

'Max and Jack, get over here,' Pete called to them both. 'What is this nonsense about an overpass?'

Jack looked at Will. 'We discussed it, on the way here at the same time as the vadium.'

'I've discussed so much my head is spinning. I do recall the conversation but we never said we'd do it.'

Jack looked disappointed.

'Why do you want an overpass anyway? What difference is it going to make to you?'

'It would take Max and me much less time to get to the vennis vackets and we could spend more time playing.'

Pete rolled his eyes while Will knew he needed to step outside of his own issues and follow the letter C in their mission.

'Could you all excuse Pat and me for a moment?'

Pete, Peg, Jack and Max all nodded.

By this stage Amy had wandered over, followed closely by Hugh and Reece. Will saw them and hand signalled them over. 'We need to have a team meeting.'

'What's up Will?'

'It's your blooming ring of calmness that's haunting me.'

Amy held it up. 'If you look through it maybe it will make you calm.'

'Save it Ames.'

'What's the problem?'

'Hugh, when Jack and I were together earlier, before I suggested the vadium, he suggested an overpass that joins all the structures here together. That idea went by the wayside when the vadium idea took over.'

'So?'

'The problem is the way Pete relayed the message as he understood it. Construct an Overpass. Do any of you get where I am coming from?'

Pat was amazed. 'Well done Will. Cyril did say the clues would present.'

Will rolled his eyes at Pat. 'So here's what we've got.

'A is for Assemble the Date Wall which is starting to take form.' Will pointed at it.

'B is for, I have no clue what.'

Amy and Reece turned and faced each other at the same time.

'Reece are you thinking what I'm thinking?'

Reece nodded with a smile, 'I think so Amy.'

'What is it?' asked Will.

'B is for Blast. I know where to get the object to blast. I just haven't worked out what we need to blast.'

'I have.'

They all looked at Reece.

'When Amy and I went to help Hillary back in the Lava Hi House she had the largest ven-la-roc you've ever seen. She refers to it as her treasure. It is so big and heavy it would take two of us to lift it. When Will and I were at the sinkhole that has turned to a mound of lava, the geyser that Amy came out of lasted for a short while then dried up. We created the geyser in the first place by throwing lots of small ven-la-rocs into the sinkhole. I wonder what would happen if we threw that one almighty one in?'

'Brilliant! I can add to that. When I was caught in what we now know is a cavity under where the Date Wall was, the ground was cool but the roof was hot. Now it makes sense. There is water under there, I don't know why... I just know it, but only the large ven-la-roc could blast through that cavity and set the water free.'

'So Venus could have a geyser in the middle of it?'

'I wouldn't say geyser, Will, but a fountain. We want water to flow continually, not to blast, erupt and dry up.'

'Wow Amy and Reece, you've been holding back.'

'No, Pat. We've only just pieced it together.'

'Okay, okay. Now;

'A is for Assemble, and we've started that.

'B is for Blast which is blast the geyser or fountain. The problem is how do we get into the Lava Hi House to get the ven-la-roc?'

Everyone stood silent. It was an excellent point Will had made.

Amy rubbed her foot on the ground and felt something move in her heel. She had not paid attention to it for so long because it had been there a while. She sat on the ground and released her secret compartment, producing three keys. As she held them up, each beamed a ray of light.

'I didn't know you had those with you,' said Will.

'Yes. I keep them in this secret compartment in the heel of my shoe.'

'Three? When we got home you had just two.'

'When Hugh was trying to fix my lavalorry I found the third one on the ground. I must have dropped one when we flew over Venus on our way back to Earth.'

Will's mouth dropped open.

'What are the keys for?' asked Hugh.

'They opened the airflow in the statues on Mercury.'

'Why do you still have them then?'

'I never got around to giving them back.'

'The light from them... I wonder if that is the letter D for Discover in our alphabet puzzle?' mused Pat.

'It could be. D is for Discover. Cyril mentioned we need to Discover an additional function of something we already have.'

'That's right!' said Will. 'You asked who had the object. He said you'd be the best one to work that out.'

'What lock can you use the keys for?' asked Reece. 'Leave that to me.'

'What teamwork. I'm proud of all of you,' said Pat.

Pete looked over to see the team laughing and conversing. He, Peg, Jack and Max wandered over. 'You look happy. Will we construct this overpass?'

'Pete, we think that's a great idea.'

'Good. We're in if you are in.'

Will, Pat, Amy, Hugh and Reece all agreed.

'How shall we start?'

'To Construct an overpass that runs between all four structures and then a circular road that allows the nicbeings to go from, for example, north to east without traversing across the middle is going to need a fair few long solid pipes. There is a nicbeing among us here right now who is able to get such a thing.'

Everyone looked around to Jack.

'Who me? I don't have any long solid pipes.'

'Yes you do Jack, I've seen them.'

Jack thought about it. 'Oh! In the scrap heap.'

'Uh huh,' was all Will answered.

'What's the plan from here Will?'

CHAPTER FOURTEEN
IT'S A BLAST

'Pete, do you know a channel on the two way we can all tune to? One that Henry wouldn't use?'

'I think you're pretty safe there Will. Henry is so ancient he doesn't use a two way.'

'Good then, show us how to do it.'

Pete, Peg, Jack and Max all had hand held two ways but Will, Pat, Amy, Hugh and Reece were relying on the ones in their lavalorries. The team Jack had brought over with the liquid lava were assembling the Date Wall. It was being erected perfectly based on the instructions Will had outlined for them.

'Max, go to those three lavalorries and channel the two ways in please?'

'Okay Paanic.'

Max skipped to complete the allocated task while Jack turned the volume on his two way up. He had it right down so he could hear the previous conversation.

'Jaaaaack, are you there come in. Over.'

Jack looked embarrassed

'Jack, I'm calling you now answer me. Over.'

He shyly put the two way to his mouth.

'What is it Maanic? Over.'

'Jack, I've been trying to reach you for ages so where are you? Don't tell me you're playing vennis again. Over.'

'No Maanic, I'm not.'

'I'm tired of chasing you to do your work. You get back here at once.'

Jack rolled his eyes while everyone stood around listening to the conversation between him and his maanic, Molly.

'I was doing it and you didn't like what I was doing. Over.'

'Jack, don't you dare argue with me. I asked you to wait until I finished what I was doing but you were too impatient and took off to ride the Slava Sleigh.'

'She doesn't miss much,' said Jack quietly but he forgot he had his finger on the talk button.

'I heard that Jack. You get back here at once. Over.'

'Okay, I'm on my way. Over.'

'She doesn't sound too happy Jack.'

'What gave it away Peg?'

'I'd be the same if Max ran off.'

'Okay, I get it, but sometimes it's so boring over there and I want to do different things.'

Pete put his hand on Jack's shoulder. 'How about we give you a lift back to the twin Slava Slopes and talk to Molly about those poles on the scrap heap.'

'That would be great.'

By this stage Max had arrived back. Jack got in Max's lorry and Pete and Peg took off behind.

'Okay Will; now it's just us, where to?' asked Hugh.

'We need to complete B before C gets underway so let's head for the Hi House.'

'While going to the Hi House is the obvious first stop,' said Pat, 'don't you think we need a plan?'

'Probably, and I'm guessing you have one?'

'I have part of it.'

'I think I have a plan,' offered Hugh.

'Let's hear it.'

Hugh shared his plan while the others listened and filled in the bits Hugh was unsure of.

'Okay have we got it?'

'We've got it,' they answered and to the lavalorries they went. Pat travelled alone, followed by Will and Hugh then behind Amy and Reece.

Hugh saw Will was preoccupied. 'What's up?'

'Oh I...' He ran his hand through his hair. 'I'm trying to work out if there would be any way of getting the magnifier back while we're here.'

'Are you mad?' asked Hugh. 'We'll be lucky to get the oversized rock out without being noticed. Do you think you're going to rock up to Henry and Zac and say, *hey dudes please give my magnifier back*?'

'I know it's not like they'll just hand it back.'

'Trust me Will. I've been there. Once you get hold of that thing it makes you feel invincible. It's not as big a deal for you because it's yours. Anyway on this occasion let's stick to one thing.'

They travelled the rest of the journey in silence.

Henry had worked himself up into such a state his mind went blank. When he could think again, he busied himself in his secret room trying to get the fire rock machine fired up and finally got it going.

Before blasting at any targets he thought it wise to check on the progress of the new Date Wall. It was not hard to see for now it had been erected and there looked to be other structures going up on each side of it. He couldn't work out exactly what these were.

'There's no use firing in that direction. It's new and if it doesn't get completed no nicbeing will care. They've not lived with it so they'll find it easier to live without it. I need to fire at something that will hurt them, a structure the nicbeings depend on. Hee hee hee.' Henry had an evil chuckle to himself.

'What's funny Henry? I recognise that evil chuckle.'

The voice took Henry by surprise. 'Hillary, what are you doing up here?'

'You have to stop what you are doing. This will bring us undone.'

'No it won't.'

'It will. Please listen to me. You've held control for too long and believe me the herds are getting restless. Have a look on our doorstep. There are so many nicbeings out there fighting and dodging shovels, spades and pellets not to mention your burning lava rocks they've forgotten which side they are on.'

'Good, my plan is working.'

'Our home is being destroyed.'

'Who cares? It's old anyway.'

Hillary lost her cool. 'Why can you not see this?'

'I don't want to change. I don't care how much anger I cause, I just want it my way and if you knew what was good for you, you'd get out of my way.'

Hillary walked around in front of him with her index finger pointed. 'Don't do it Henry. I know what you're planning and I strongly suggest you don't do it.'

Henry did not respond as Hillary left the room.

The three lavalorries arrived at the Lava Hi House to nicbeings punching each other, and spades and shovels being thrown while the nicbeings dodged a continual flow of burning lava rocks.

'I didn't realise the fighting was this bad Will. Over.'

'Ames, me either. I suggest you lead the way since you know where the secret entrance is.'

Amy led the three lorries around the back where not as much fighting was taking place. 'I think if we are clever about this, we might not get noticed.'

'Speak for yourself Amy.'

'Sorry Pat, I forgot you are a crowd gatherer.'

They pulled their lorries up near a group of others.

'We all need to stick to the plan... got it?' said Will.

'Got it. And take it easy. We're a team.'

'Sorry Pat.'

Amy led them to the entrance of the volcano which was an open arch. Inside there was nothing to see except rocks. Pat and Reece waited at the entrance. Pat sat back on his hind legs and Reece knelt to pat him.

'We'll stay here on watch, so hurry.'

'We'll be as quick as we can Pat.'

Amy showed Will and Hugh the door which was the same size as the one they originally used to enter the Hi House. 'Here's the door to the tunnel. Notice there are three key holes in the lock.'

'I hope those keys open it,' wished Hugh.

Amy got the three keys out and handed one each to Will and Hugh. They crouched by the door. Each put a key into a hole then turned. Nothing happened.

'Okay, let's rotate right and each try the next hole.'

On the next try the door unlocked. They noticed the very narrow tunnel Amy had described to them.

'Ames, you go first. You know where the rock is.'

'It's at the entrance of the trapdoor. I hope it's in the same position. I'll have to roll it into this tunnel.'

'Once you get it here, I'll help you roll it to the end,' said Will.

'And I'll be here ready to lift it out of this tunnel.'

'It's heavy, Hugh.'

'Don't worry. My iron amour is strong.'

Amy crawled through the familiar tunnel and found it easier second time round. She scraped herself through and came to the trapdoor. Being as quiet as possible in case Hillary was there, she pushed her head up and slightly opened the door to peer inside. Will was at her feet and tapped his fingers on her shin. She kicked him gently away. She opened the trapdoor to see the large ven-la-roc known as the treasure.

Using all her power she rolled the rock into the passageway and shut the door behind her.

Will took the rock and rolled it as he crawled on his stomach behind it making his way through the passage with Amy just behind.

Hillary returned to her domain seconds later. She was so angry she didn't notice she'd been robbed.

Will continued pushing the rock. It was slow, but they steadily approached the end where Hugh waited.

'You're moving it along fine Will.'

'It's not too bad, Ames but you're right; it is heavy.'

Will handed the boulder to Hugh who lifted it effortlessly through the small door.

Will climbed out behind then assisted Amy. 'Got the keys Ames?'

'Sure do. There is no way I'm going without them.'

Hugh was walking to the entrance of the volcano.

'We'd better be careful out here,' cautioned Will. 'It's kind of hard to be inconspicuous.'

'Careful? I'm carrying an oversized fluoro-pink rock!'

'Let me go out first. I'll check if the coast is clear.'

'Good idea Ames.'

When Amy got out to where Pat and Reece were, Pat was holding court with a group of nicbeings who not that long ago had been fighting. She signalled for Will and Hugh to hurry.

'That's funny; who's got another joke?' asked Pat.

Reece saw Amy, Will and Hugh escape and took a firm hold of Pat's fur on the back of his neck. 'You know Pat, these nicbeings were a little busy before we interrupted them. Maybe we should leave them to get back to what they were doing.'

Pat did not get the hint. 'Don't be silly Reece. They were only fighting. Telling jokes is way better.'

'Pat my darling dog, I think we should get going.'

By this stage the rock was loaded into the lorry with Will and Hugh and they had taken off. Amy was waving madly to hurry Reece and Pat along. She jumped into her lorry and Reece and Pat ran madly and both got into Pat's lorry.

'Is everyone okay? Over.'

'Yes Will, we're all fine. If Pat wasn't such a crowd pleaser we may not have gotten away so easily.'

'I had to address my adoring public.'

'Oh and did I add modest also. Over.'

'Do you think Hillary knows, Amy?'

'It's hard to say. I'm pretty sure eventually she'll notice. That rock is her treasure.'

'Let's hope her treasure works for us.'

'We're just about to find out.'

On arriving at the mound of lava they saw a couple of childnics having running competitions across the top of the lava mound.

'I hope they don't fall in,' said Pat.

'Not likely,' said Reece. 'It was solid when Will and I were last here rescuing Amy.'

Will and Hugh carried the rock to the edge of the solid lava mound.

'Hey childnics, get off there,' called Will.

'You can't make us.'

'Yes I can.'

'No you can't.'

Pat saw Will's tactics were not working so he moved in. 'Come over here and tell me a joke.'

The childnics looked at each and then at Pat.

'I'll race you; the first one who gets to that area over there gets to tell the first joke. Ready on your marks, one, two, three—go.'

The childnics raced to where Pat was to sit around him chatting, asking questions and telling jokes.

Amy and Reece watched. 'He's a marvel Amy.'

'He really is. I don't know what I'd do without him.'

'Okay Hugh, have you got it?' asked Will.

'Ready when you are.'

'Ready, set—go.'

The rock was tossed with enough height to hit the very top of the mound. A large crack appeared.

'Nothing's happening Will.'

'Wait.'

The rock sank into the mound and although the reaction took time a tiny flow of water came from the middle of it. It was not strong and was not constant but it was much the same as a flow from a bubbler.

'That's not what I expected,' said Reece to Amy.

'Me either.'

One of the group of childnics that surrounded Pat saw the very small flow so jumped up and ran to it. Chances were it was the first time that childnic had ever seen water. The team casually walked and stood beside the tiny flow of water looking down at it.

'I don't think that was the desired result.'

'Well done Pat for stating the obvious,' said Hugh.

'This amount of water won't keep half a nicbeing going, let alone a whole planet.'

'Clearly not. You can barely see it and the flow is not consistent.'

'I don't get it. Cyril gave us the letter B, and we've done what we thought without the right result.'

'Amy, not everything works out as you imagine it.'

'Now we've done what we thought we had to for B, we should get project C underway,' said Will.

'Will, Will are you there? Over.' Will was not quite at his lorry when he heard the page. He hurried the last few steps. 'Come in Pete.'

'We're at the twin Slava Slopes and we've been talking to Molly. She insists she meets you and hears of your plans before she releases the poles.'

Will went silent. They were all gathered around. 'Pat, what could I say that the others haven't already?'

'Sometimes you just have to meet people to put their minds at rest.'

'Okay, Pete. We're on our way.'

'See you soon. Over and out.'

'Okay team, off we go again. It's such a shame about the lack of water.'

'We'll try to fix it later,' said Amy. 'I'll go with you.'

Amy hopped in with Will, Reece and Hugh together and Pat on his lonesome.

CHAPTER FIFTEEN
MEET MOLLY

'Are you tired Will? It's been big.'

'Not big Ames, epic, and we've a lot more to do.'

'I'm a glass is half full chick. So far we've assembled the Date Wall, made an attempt at a fountain, are on the way to construct the overpass and have discovered the additional function of the keys. It's as easy as ABC.' She started laughing.

'Who'd have thought the Mercury keys would have helped us so much?'

'I would,' said Amy as she put her hand in the air.

'Of course, you're a glass is half full girl.'

Amy playfully stuck her tongue out at Will.

'Now we're headed for the twin Slava Slopes I hope we get a turn at the Mosaic Moveator.'

'I don't know Will. Molly is the boss. She sounded fierce when we heard her with Jack on the two way.'

They pulled their lorries up just beside Pete and Peg's and entered the twin Slava Slopes where they were greeted by Jack and Max.

'Will, your big moment has arrived; we have to ride the Mosaic Moveator.'

'I can't wait.'

Hugh whispered to Reece, 'I'm super glad we're here. I need to get up high and get some air into me. I'm feeling really dehydrated.'

Amy overheard. 'Even after that small flow of water?'

'Flow of water where?'

Max and Jack stared with their beady eyes but no one said anything.

'What water flow? I've never seen water on Venus. We've learned about it so I know what it is but I've never seen it."

'Max, it's so small, it's not worth mentioning. It mightn't even be there when we get back to it.'

'Where was it Pat?'

'Where the Date Wall-cum-Sinkhole-cum-Lava Mound once was.'

'How?' questioned Max.

'Before we get into too many questions just accept it's tiny and the flow is inconsistent.'

Max looked at Jack. 'What fun we're going to have with that,' he said as he rubbed his hands together.

'Jack, the Mosaic Moveator remember.'

'Oh yeah sorry Will. Come on over here.'

Jack led the way to a small shallow pond of lava and both he and Max jumped in. It came up to their ankles. Some of the lava had splashed out onto Amy.

'Jack,' she said, annoyed.

'Don't worry; this lava's been treated so it won't hurt. Get in and give it a go.'

'What are we doing?'

'If you want to ride on the Mosaic Moveator you need a pair of moots. I don't know what you call them back on Earth but they are things that fit on your feet.'

Amy giggled. 'We call them boots.'

Pat did not put his paws in the pond.

'Pat, what's stopping you?' asked Jack.

'I have four paws. Will it work the same for me?'

'I don't know. No dog ever rode before. Try.'

That was all Pat needed and he bounded in.

'Now what?' said Will.

'When you get out this treated lava will dry and you'll have your moots. A unique feature of this one of the twin Slava Slopes is there is one strip on the side here where the lava flows upwards. If this feature wasn't here we'd not be able to get to the top of the twin Slava Slopes.'

They stood at the base and watched the lava running upwards.

'That is impressive,' said Hugh.

'We think so, but we did not create this masterpiece. It's natural,' said Jack. 'Now, to get on you edge your way into the upflow, the moots will grab on and up you go.'

Jack and Max demonstrated. 'Will, you should go first; it was you who wanted to ride this.'

Will's moots latched on and up he went. The others followed quickly.

'Hold on, it's easy to overbalance,' said Amy.

'There's nothing to hold onto,' said Reece.

Jack called out, 'Don't worry your moots will stop you from falling.'

Reece turned back to Pat. 'How are you going with the four paws?'

'Amazingly well, especially when the lava flow pulls my paws in four different directions.'

'I'm having that same problem except with two feet. I'll probably be able to do the splits after this.'

They laughed at Reece's comment and continued to enjoy their ride on the Mosaic Moveator.

Henry had a keen eye out and could see the single file of them going up the side of twin Slava Slope One.

'Henry, Henry.'

He took a moment to get up from where he was and go to the top of the staircase to answer. 'What is it Hillary?'

'The large ven-la-roc, my treasure; it's been stolen.'

'Really?' was all he said and he did not wait to hear Hillary's reply but returned to his viewing platform. What he had seen now made sense. A flash of florescent pink had caught his eye as he watched it being flung into the sinkhole. At first he had no idea what it was but now Hillary had provided the answer.

How could they have gotten that?

Henry was furious his Hi House had been broken into. Hillary might know how they got in, but there was no time for explanations; they had stolen the treasured ven-la-roc and had to pay.

Now's the time, he decided as he scurried to his secret room. He set fire to the enormous lava rock in the cradle. He carefully calculated his aim then fired. The rock propelled from one side of Venus to the other, directly at twin Slava Slope one, where the single file was almost at the top. To make things worse, standing at the top were Pete, Peg and Molly and they saw everything happen in slow motion.

The rock skimmed past Pat, who was last in line, and it singed some of the fur on his butt. It bounced off a small incline in the mountain and landed at Pete, Peg and Molly's feet where the lava flow caught it and began to roll it down the mountain.

'Get off that Mosaic Moveator at once,' screamed Molly.

'We can't until we get to the top, Maanic, you know that.'

Pat realised Molly had panicked for everyone's safety.

170

'How dare Henry launch at all of us, especially when our businesses are the two biggest users of his products. That old so and so, how dare he?'

When Molly roared she was pretty scary; she could rival Henry with her temper.

Once at the top, Jack led everyone over to Molly.

'Everyone inside so we're sheltered from Henry's next attempt,' she ordered.

'How do you know there'll be one Molly?'

'Pete, believe me, I know Henry really well and look what's coming at us.'

Pete turned to see the next boulder blazing through the air. This time it hit the other Slava Slope and injured nicbengs working there.

'What are you going to do?'

'Not another word, everyone inside.'

Not game to defy Molly they rushed inside.

'Maanic, this is Will, Amy and Pat, from Earth and Hugh and Reece from Mercury,' said Jack.

Molly held out her gloved hand in greeting.

'Molly, it's so hot,' said Amy. 'Why wear gloves?'

Molly looked at Jack who shrugged, then back at Amy.

'I've never asked,' said Jack. 'Maanic why do you wear gloves?'

'I like to protect my hands and this is the best way.'

Pete took a look outside. 'Now they're here Molly and Henry's firing with force, do you want to ask them?'

'Ask us what?' enquired Will.

'I need to know why you want to construct the overpass and how you intend to do it.'

Another rock hit outside as the vibration went through them.

171

Will looked at Pat and mouthed, 'You should probably answer.'

'Molly,' said Pat.

She stared, and Pat picked up on her surprise.

'Yes Molly, I can talk.'

'I can hear that now,' she answered.

'We want to construct the overpass firstly because Will and Jack discussed it and secondly because it's part of our mission while we're here. We intend to do it using the poles I'm told you have in your scrap heap.'

'How do you know?'

'I've seen them,' said Will.

'Of course you have, when you were riding the Slava Sleigh with Jack.'

'Peg and I would help with the project,' said Pete.

Jack was nervous about Molly's decision he blurted out, 'They've found water.'

Molly, Pete and Peg's eyes all nearly popped out of their sockets.

Pat cringed as he didn't think it was worth mentioning.

'It's true, they found water where the Date Wall used to be,' said Jack.

'We have water on Venus?' Molly stared at Will.

Will wanted to bury his head. 'It's a very tiny flow and inconsistent. I'm not sure it would even be there if you went now.'

'Water is water. Venus's oceans dried up long ago.'

'We knew that Pete. We thought we'd found an answer but it turns out we didn't get the result we hoped. It's disappointing as it was one of our missions.'

'How many missions in total do you have?'

'Seven.'

'Seven,' echoed Molly. 'How many are completed?'

'Really only one is complete, one is under construction, one hasn't resulted to our expectations and with luck we'll get another underway if you allow us to use those poles.'

'That's confident of you Will.'

'Come on Maanic, for goodness sake. I hate how you are so stubborn, it's just like that stupid Henry.'

Molly's face changed she looked at Jack with daggers in her eyes. 'Don't you dare say that Jack.'

'All right but we're wasting time. Can we please use the poles and get on with it?'

Molly paused. 'Take them, use them all.'

Everyone cheered. They hastened down the Mosaic Moveator and got safely to the bottom in between Henry's bursts of burning rocks. The poles were loaded onto each of the lorries strategically orchestrated by Pete and they moved swiftly away from the twin Slava Slopes leaving Molly behind.

Molly got to all of her workers and told them to down tools as it was getting too dangerous to continue. Instead she divided them and sent each group to a different section to go and assist constructing the new overpass. Once the last worker had left the mountain she turned and saw a burning lava rock hit and completely destroy her home that she had worked so hard for and which was so dear to her. Molly watched in shock, unable to believe what she had just witnessed.

'That's it Henry; it's time for you to go down,' she said through gritted teeth.

Will and the team drove the poles to where the new Date Wall was. There they were met by many of Pete's nicbeings who unloaded their lorries and began constructing the overpass. Will remembered to grab his sack of not so precious gems from the secret glove box he had them hidden in.

'Things are so much easier when there is a team of nicbeings working with you.'

'Without them, I'm not sure we'd have been able to do what we've done so far,' said Pat.

'I think we still need to concentrate on the Date Wall. It may be up but it's not finished.' Will held up the sack full of not so precious gems. 'Come on Amy, I'm pretty sure you'll have things to help with this.'

While they all stood in front of the new Date Wall with the vadium seating still under construction on both sides, they admired the nicbeings' handiwork and noted the short amount of time it took them.

'Let's sit on the ground over here and work out how to attack this. I'm sure Henry knows we're here and will aim in our direction soon.'

Will was first to sit then the others joined him. He laid out his collection of not so precious gems on the ground. 'Come on Amy out with them.'

'Oh Will, I was hoping to take at least one home.'

'Wishful thinking Ames.'

She laid hers out.

'You have only eleven gems and Will has twelve,' said Pat.

'I know. That was all I could find.'

Hugh had been studying the wall very closely. 'I think I've worked out what to do.'

'Go ahead. I'm happy to follow your instructions.'

Hugh was elated by the comment from Will. He'd always felt on the back foot when Will was involved.

'To click these gems into place we'll need all of us except for Pat who will monitor the progress from below. Amy, you and I will go up one end and Will, you and Reece on the other.'

They listened intently. Hugh had really thought this out.

'See how the stadium seating is in progress and it's providing steps for us to climb the walls on both ends?' He pointed. 'We need to be as quick as we can so we can get down the same way we got up.'

'Spot on,' Will agreed.

'We'll need a set of gems for the aquanic side and for the libnic side.'

'That's the part that's going to bring us undone.'

'Why, Amy?'

'I have only eleven, remember?'

'Okay, let's sort them and see which one's missing.'

Reece laid the identical sets side by side and there was one heart-shaped gem missing.

'Wow, we're on Venus that is supposed to be the planet of love and the missing gem is heart-shaped.'

'Good observation Amy, I never thought of that.'

Hugh cut in, 'We've got to hurry this through so Will, take these and Reece, you take those, Amy, you take that group and I'll take these.'

They each picked up a group of gems and began their climb on each side of the wall. Once at the top, they had to straddle the wall and edge their way into the middle of it. Amy went first from her side while Reece was first from hers. They met in the middle then stretched their heads over to the side the libnic was on and clicked the stones into place, moving outwards. Hugh was right behind Amy as Will was right behind Reece except they clicked the stones into place on the aquanic side of the wall. Once all the stones were clicked in, they made their way to their respective ends and climbed down the under-construction vadium seats and safely to the ground.

'It looks really good.'

'Thanks Pat but something is not right.'

'I feel the same way,' said Amy, nodding to Will.

'Of course something is not right about it; you're missing a gem.'

'We know that, but there's something more. We'll have to try and work it out.'

They all stood there staring at the one gem missing from the aquanic side of the wall.

'You know Marky did tell us that where each hump meets is one of Earth's months,' said Pat, 'so if you look at it like this, where the first hump meets indicates January and that is marked with a cone shaped gem but where the second hump meets indicates February and that should be marked with a heart shaped gem, of course the only one we are missing.'

'So?'

'Will, on Earth February is known as the month of love. Isn't it ironic that here on Venus the planet of love that is the only gem missing.'

Amy pondered Pat's comment. 'Valentine's Day is in February!'

'Yes Amy it is.'

'Will, Will, over here.'

Will heard his named being called but couldn't work out where it was coming from.

'Will, over here, it's me, Molly.'

Will saw Molly tearing towards them in her lavalorry.

Once she was close she hopped out and admired the Date Wall. 'Wow, you've done a sterling job of this Date

Wall.' She studied it a bit longer. 'There's a gem missing.'

'We know that. Why were you looking for us?'

Molly ignored Will's question because she wanted some of her own answers. 'Do those gems on the top where the humps meet appear on both sides?'

'Yes, they do.'

'What shape is missing?'

Will was a little suspicious with the way the questions were being asked and the fact she had not surrendered the reason she was here in the first place.

'Why? Do know where we might find it?'

She didn't answer directly. 'I'm intrigued by you finding water. What did you do to discover it?'

Amy cut in. 'Molly, we found such a little amount it's probably dried up and not worth discussing.'

'if you won't talk about it I'll ask Will.'

'He's right there, so ask him,' retorted Amy.

Will looked at Amy unsure of how to react. 'Sorry Molly, the best person to explain is Amy. If she can't help you I certainly can't.'

Molly fiddled with the glove on her right hand. She then leaned over and put each of her hands on Amy's shoulders and started to shake her. 'You must tell me Amy,' Molly yelled as the others watched on.

CHAPTER SIXTEEN
HIDDEN IN THE
GLOVE

Zac was getting bored with propelling rocks from the lower level of the Hi House. He had no idea what was going on and his inquisitive mind was getting the better of him. The nicbeings around him were not his concern; he had bigger targets like Will and the magnifier. Henry was the only one that would know where both those things were so Zac left his station with everything open and made the trek to the top.

'Henry, where are you?'

'I'm here Zac, in my private area. Come into the glass room where we view Venus.'

Zac noted a small secret door and Henry just inside.

'What are you doing?' asked Zac as he entered and saw the magnifier half sticking out of Henry's pocket.

'Is there something wrong with you? You can see what I'm doing can't you?'

'Firing rocks.'

'Gee, you're clever.'

'But at who?'

Henry gave Zac a blank look. 'You have to ask?'

Zac stuck his head in beside where Henry's was to see the target Henry was aiming at. 'Is that the new Date Wall?'

'Well done Zac. Did it take all your brains to work it out?'

Zac didn't know what to say so he stood silent and watched Henry.

'I'm going to knock them all out in one hit, the structure and those other ones like you.'

Zac was wary but he took a closer look at where Henry was aiming.

'Henry, there looks to be more than the two humans and their dog standing there in front of the Date Wall. I mean, the libnic that runs the twin Slava Slopes also seems to be there.'

'You mean Molly.'

'I guess so. You've only shown me an old picture but that libnic has gloves on and you did tell me she always wears her gloves.'

Henry pushed Zac's head out of the way to get a closer view and sure enough he saw Molly with her hands on one of the humans. Henry was never good with names and faces.

'So it is. Well spotted. That is Molly.'

'I keep telling you Henry; we make a great team,' said Zac as he playfully pushed Henry.

Henry looked at him sternly but did not comment.

'What are you going to do now?'

'I'm going to fire at that new wall. With a bit of luck those stupid humans will get knocked out on the way.'

'You're not worried about that Molly libnic?'

Henry thought for a while. He lowered his eyes but soon lifted them again. 'Nah, there's too much history.'

Zac had no idea what Henry meant by that and did not care enough to ask. He was fixated on the pending explosion and the magnifier in Henry's pocket.

'Okay here goes.' Henry got up and pulled the big old stiff lever back then let it go. The flaming lava rock soared into the atmosphere.

Pat was watching Molly shake Amy when the rock heading for them caught his eye. He ran directly into Molly and Amy causing a domino effect on Will, Hugh and Reece as they all felt the wind from the passage of the rock. The rock ploughed directly into the face of the libnic etched into the wall then broke into millions of little pieces that scattered everywhere. Some of the embers were still in flames but the force had caused most to extinguish.

The way Will had been shoved had him half sitting up with Molly and Amy in his lap. He had turned to watch the wall for damage when he saw the mouth excrete something small that was propelled to the ground. The others were trying to recover but Will hastily jumped up, went over and grabbed it. It was two very small square mirrors hinged together.

Each mirror was approximately 3cm x 3cm and they looked quite ordinary. Will wondered if anything had come out of the mouth of the aquanic on the other side of the wall so he used the small doorway that had been allowed between the wall and the vadium seats to sneak through and have a look.

Sure enough the same kind of mirror was sticking out of the aquanic mouth. By the time Will walked back through to the others, he thought no one had noticed him missing. He swiftly stuffed the mirrors into his pocket and went to help everyone back to their feet.

Molly was not finished with Amy. She was dishevelled so got and up and made a quick attempt to brush herself down, checked she still had both gloves on then leaped at Amy again.

This time Amy was faster than she was and went to grab Molly's right hand but instead of getting her fingers she got the glove and wrenched it off her. Molly fell face down with her arm and hand above her head. A sparkle caught Amy's eye.

'Molly, that's the...' Amy was lost for words.

The others gathered round and saw what Amy had seen.

'Molly, your ring, it's exactly the same as...' Amy was so taken aback she still couldn't get the words out.

Reece noticed and put her hands over her mouth. 'Amy is that the...?' asked Reece as she shook her index finger at Molly's finger.

'Molly, your ring is exactly the same as Hillary's.'

As soon as those words left Amy's lips a ray of light shone from the ring. The beam lasted only seconds then faded.

Molly through all this had her face down. Now she looked up, bent her hand up so she could see the ring was still there then pushed herself up on her knees. 'No it's not. I don't know what you're talking about.'

Amy still had Molly's glove until she snatched it and replaced it on her hand.

'Now tell me... how did you get into that Hi House?'

'Molly, the ring.'

'Never mind about the ring. How did you get in?'

Amy was miffed, but she shook her head and decided to answer Molly's question. 'We got in through a trapdoor.'

'The trapdoor?'

'I don't know if it was *the* trapdoor but it was *a* trapdoor.'

'Amy, you be honest with me, how hard was it to get in to?'

Amy did not want to answer any further questions so she shrugged.

Always calm in a not so calm situation, Pat thought he might have a solution. 'Molly, bullying Amy for clues on trying to get into the Hi House is not going to work. While I don't know where the trapdoor is your sonnic Jack and his best friendnic Max do have an answer on how to get into the Lava Hi House using the vennis vackets.'

'Oh really?'

'Indeed Molly. And as a tip, if you ever lay as much as a finger on Amy again I may not be as cooperative as I was in getting you out of the line of fire.'

'Oh really?'

'Molly, I think you are most likely a lovely libnic and you've done a great job with your twin Slava Slopes and your sonnic Jack but as a word of advice I would suggest you learn to control that temper and I'm sure you would get further quicker.'

Molly was not happy about being spoken to like that by a dog so she walked off in a huff. Just clear of where they were she held her two way to her mouth.

'Jaaaacccccckkkkkkkk,' she yelled into it.

Without waiting for a reply she again yelled, 'Jaaaaaaaaaaaaacccccccccccckkk.'

'I'm here. What do you want?'

'Jack, get Max and come to the Wasteland. It's time I tried out this vennis you keep raving about.'

Jack was so excited he couldn't believe what he'd heard. He ran to Pete and Peg and told them and then grabbed Max and headed for the vennis vacket. Molly stood tapping her toe, waiting as patiently as she could.

Will caught Amy staring at Molly's regloved hand so he whispered to her, 'What is it Amy?'

Reece, Hugh and Pat all moved in and together they moved farther away from where Molly waited.

Amy rubbed her eyes and her hands were shaking.

'Don't worry Ames we're here with you,' said Will as he patted her back for moral support.

'She is scary.'

'Sure is Amy,' agreed Reece.

Amy continued to fidget, holding her fingers to her mouth.

'Out with it Amy; what is it?'

'That amethyst ring on Molly's finger is a perfect match to the one Hillary is wearing.'

'That can't be right.'

'It is Will, I swear Amy is right. I've seen Hillary's ring. When Amy and I were helping her Amy asked about it. Hillary said there was another but then said she didn't know what happened to it,' said Reece.

'Amy and Reece, so what you're saying is Molly is somehow related to Hillary and Henry?' said Pat.

'We don't know how or even if they're related but there is a connection there.'

Jack and Max arrived.

'Maanic, come and we'll show you vennis,' said Jack.

'I don't have time for playing, but they tell me,' she said as she looked in the team's direction, 'that you too can get me into the Lava Hi House.'

'Why would you want to go there?'

'Because I want to. How do you get me there?'

'Molly, it was a fluke when I flung Will and his gang into the Hi House,' said Max. 'There was a garage left open and I've only seen it open on that occasion.'

'Come, Max, surely you and Jack know what to do.'

Pat engaged his super vision. 'Ah excuse me.'

'We don't have time for you Pat,' replied Molly as she turned and pointed her back towards him.

'Really? What I'm about to say will help you.'

She turned back. 'Go on.'

'There's a door below the garages that's open. It doesn't look big enough to fit a lavalorry through but if there is a safe way to fling a nicbeing then you will easily fit through it.'

Jack was astonished. 'How can you see that Pat?'

'It will sound absurd but I have super seeing and hearing.'

'It does sound absurd, so much so we're going to take your word for it. Up to now you've done everything you were going to do and thanks to you all the overpass is almost complete.'

'Jack, not sure if you've noticed your vadium is up.'

Jack's face lit up. 'I can't wait to try it out and yes I did notice.'

'Now is not the time Jack.'

'Okay Maanic, I got it.'

Jack and Max made plans, then Max took off to the other vacket while Jack walked a nervous Molly through the steps of getting into the Wasteland vacket.

Pat returned to the conference with the others.

'What's so special about that ring? Just that it matches Hillary's?' said Will.

'When we were with Hillary I commented on it. She said there were only two faultless stones ever found, and I do remember this part. She said one was for her and *one for my...* she never finished the sentence. She cut it off and moved onto the next topic.'

'That's different to the story Marky from the Date Wall told us,' said Hugh. 'Do you remember, Will? He said rumour has it Hillary and Henry had a daugnic but she died.'

'That's right.'

'I wonder if it's true.'

Reece noticed Amy looking odd. 'Amy what is it?'
'When I grabbed the glove and exposed the ring did you see the beam of light?'

Reece didn't answer but put her hands to her mouth. The others had caught on.

'Amy, did you hear what you said?' asked Pat.

'All I said was....' She stopped mid-sentence, 'I exposed the other amethyst.'

'Bravo Amy, you've just uncovered the E clue.'

'OMG, there is a connection. We need to get the Hi House pronto.'

'Why Amy?' asked Pat.

'I think there is about to be a showdown like Venus has never seen.'

'You mean like *Henry* has never seen.'

'Not sure Will but we've assembled, blasted, constructed, discovered and exposed so there's just one left; Find!'

'You think the answer is over there.'

'There's more chance than here.'

Everyone looked up in time to see Molly flung from the vackets and fly over their heads.

'I agree Amy; if we don't get there we may never *Find*.'

'You're the logistics man Will, what's the best way?'

'I think we need to arm from all sides. Pat, you and I will two way Jack and Max and get them to fling us as they have just done with Molly. Amy, you, Reece and Hugh take two lorries and go in through the secret door. That way we can cause a distraction to get Hillary out of her domain.'

'Okay Will, see you there.'

'Oh and Amy, for goodness sake get me a ven-la-roc. I'm the only one who hasn't tried one.'

Amy reached into her pocket and threw one of her last two at Will. 'This one is on me.'

'Wait up, I haven't tried them either.'

'Okay Pat, come here and I'll fetch yours from around your neck before we go up in the vacket.'

Will did as he promised and they both enjoyed an energy boost and a taste sensation. Will then went to the last lorry left and got Jack on the two way.

'Hey Jack buddy, come in.'

'What's up Will?'

'Yeah what's up Will?' echoed Max.

'Pat and I need a bullseye shot into the Hi House.'

'What's rocking over there that everyone suddenly needs to go?'

'Not sure at this stage.'

'Well, if you're going so are we.'

Will did not say a thing but Jack got on the two way.

'Max, I'm going to fling us all to you then you can shoot us in. You're the one with the best aim.'

'I've not missed yet.'

'I know and that is why we are coming to you.'

Jack lowered the vacket to capture Will and Pat while Amy and Reece took off in one lorry and Hugh close behind in the other.

'Hold on Will, almost there.'

'We're holding.'

The vacket lowered and Will and Pat hopped in. This time was a little different as it had a platform in the middle for them to stand on. As Will and Pat were now without the two way they were unable to communicate with Jack or Max until they were with them, but the aquanics bantered on.

'I'm excited Max. I wonder what's going to happen?'

'Who knows? But I've always wanted to go inside the Hi House.'

'Me too. I'm going straight to the ven-la-roc room. I had one once, those things rock.'

'I didn't know you'd tried one but I'm coming with you because I want to try them. I'm always told how great they are by Paa and Maanic who had them back when they were readily available.'

Will and Pat had arrived where they needed to be. Jack hopped onto the platform with them with his remote control in one hand and his two way in the other. 'Come in Max.'

'I'm here.'

'We are pulling back now and...'

Jack flung all three across to Max's vacket which was farther away but was facing north direct to the Hi House. They landed safely.

'It's been so long since I've been a vall Max, I'd forgotten.'

'Me too. Now we have our new vadium we can train other nicbeings up to play vennis and be the vall. It would be great.'

Pat and Will waited patiently.

'Just over there Amy, you can pull up the lorry.'

Amy did that and Hugh was on their tail. Amy jumped out and the other two ran as well. 'Here's the door. Hugh, you've done the lock before but Reece, here's a key for you.'

Amy produced the three keys and like clockwork they rotated the keys until the right key went into the right lock and the latch clicked. She was mindful to get the keys back and put them safely back in her special shoe compartment. The others followed her as they all got really muddy climbing through the narrow passage way and to the trapdoor. Amy slightly pushed it open and saw Hillary's feet, so carefully shut it hoping she had not seen them.

'Come on Max we've stretched back so let's go.'

'Okay, but we only get one chance especially since we're not protected by the lavalorries.'

'I'd prefer he take a little extra time for the sake of being safe,' added Pat.

'I've got it now, hold tight... ready... one, two, three.'

The four were flung out of the vacket and were on direct course for the open door that Molly had entered only moments earlier.

Will turned to Pat. 'I hope this is a good idea.'

'Me too, Will, me too.'

CHAPTER SEVENTEEN
THE TRUTH
COMES OUT

Will, Pat, Jack and Max all made it safely into the small room and saw that was where fire-engulfed lava rocks were launched from. Jack and Max stood and watched as Will smartly disabled the machine and extinguished the fire while Pat made sure the coast was clear and used his nose to roll out any remaining boulders that were in there. There were still many nicbeings around but the shovel, spade and pellet pelting had calmed down.

'That fixes that.'

'Wow, you two really know how to stop a fight.'

'We've had a bit of practice Max but common sense would work that one out for you.'

Max was about to respond when they heard shouting.

'Henry, get down here. It's time we talked.' It was so loud it seemed every crevice in the Hi House heard it.

Henry had frozen.

'Who is that Henry?' asked Zac, who was preparing to launch another lava rock.

Henry didn't answer. He wanted to be sure his old ears heard right so he got up and went to the top of the stairs.

'Well, well, well, look who's come home,' he said as he slowly walked, taking each step one at a time.

'Henry, Henry did you hear what I heard and is that who I think it is?'

'Why don't you come and see for yourself Hillary,' the voice responded.

For the time Henry took to get down the stairs, Hillary took the same to come up from her domain. Zac stayed safely where he was aiming at another target.

'Molly dear is that you?'

'Who else would it be Maanic?'

By this stage Will, Pat, Jack and Max had slightly opened their door marked S/TSS and Amy, Reece and Hugh had come through the secret trapdoor, had filled their pockets with ven-la-roc on the way through and sat on the stairs with the trapdoor that Hillary had left wide open. They all heard Molly call Hillary *Maanic*. The most shocked was Jack, who'd had no idea.

'Molly, I am so happy finally to see you again,' said Hillary as she walked toward Molly with her arms open.

'You stay there Maanic; not another step closer.'

Hillary's face was hurt.

Henry had stepped onto the landing but had observed what happened. In the calmest voice Henry had ever used he said, 'What do you want Molly?'

She looked at him. 'How could you get so greedy and selfish? I can't believe I come from you.'

'Now just calm down Molly.'

Molly was beginning to get worked up and that comment from Henry escalated her mood. 'You swore that if I left you alone, then you'd leave me alone.'

'We have, Molly.'

'No you haven't. You not long ago blasted my twin Slava Slopes and destroyed my home. How dare you?'

Hillary put her hands to her mouth in shock and started to cry.

'Let me explain.'

'What's to explain Henry? You've destroyed me and now I will destroy you.'

Hillary's crying turned to an inconsolable sobbing. The sound was echoing through the room.

'You'll pay for this Henry.'

Henry lost it. He went to launch at Molly with his hand but tripped over an uneven stone then a shard of glass that was poking upwards from the floor slit through his left cheek. Henry screamed.

Will, Pat, Jack and Max came through one door while Amy, Reece and Hugh popped up through the trapdoor in the floor.

Hillary noticed everyone but Henry didn't as he was in agony from the pain.

'I've had it Henry. I'm here to claim what's mine.'

'Molly, it doesn't have to be this way.'

'Yes it does Hillary, he's pushed me too far this time. I used to think you two were the greatest, especially him,' she said as she pointed at Henry. 'But I don't know what happened to you, either of you. I've put up with your stupid antics, accepting deliveries of static electricity in portion boxes of which I produced the boxes for nothing. There are nicbeings dying out there of dehydration because you are too mean to share your ven-la-rocs. You tore down the Date Wall, the one and only place where there was a little bit of love, you destroyed the twin Hot Spots, tearing any dreams Pete and Peg had up and now my home has gone.'

Henry had gotten to his knees. 'It's because of them,' he said as he pointed at Will, Amy and Pat.

'They have done nothing but make all the wrong things you have done right.'

'No they haven't Molly.'

'Yes they have. Everything you've destroyed they've rebuilt. They've shown the nicbeings the way to do things regardless of you. There is only one piece of their puzzle missing and I am going to make sure they get it.'

'No Molly, please,' Henry begged.

'Why would you think I would support you now? You have done nothing but made my life hell for me and my sonnic Jack.' Molly had calmed down.

'You have a sonnic?'

'Yes Maanic, I do.'

Jack walked over to Molly who put her arm around him and hugged him.

'Henry made sure with that thoughtless blast over in the Wasteland that killed his paanic that Jack here wouldn't meet his paanic so I made sure Jack would never meet you.'

Hillary was in a trance, her eyes fixed on Jack. 'We have a grandaquanic?'

'He's standing right here.'

Henry was in tears. In fact the situation was so emotional Amy and Reece had tears in their eyes.

Will could see his magnifier in Henry's pocket and at that moment he looked up and saw Zac standing at the top of the spiral staircase. He was so shocked his mouth opened but Zac gave Will the evil stare. He was unable to show any emotion for what was going on. Will kept his eye on him as he disappeared back into wherever it was he had come from.

'Where is it Henry?'

'Where is what Molly, what do you want?'

'I want my damned heart-shaped gem Henry. It's mine, I found it, I want it because I own it. You wouldn't let me have it; pretending you were keeping it safe, but you knew all along what it was, you knew it was the missing piece of gem in the Date Wall and you knew the

Date Wall would never operate as it should without it. I'll not ask again Henry; where is it?'

Hillary had never stood up to Henry and she realised now was the time. She had the gem so she held it up.

'She's right Henry. I've stood by and not only watched you but helped you stop progress on this planet. We should be ashamed of ourselves. We have plenty... what more could we want? But even with all this wealth our life is cold and empty; hell we don't even laugh.'

Hillary walked over to Molly. 'Take this, it is rightfully yours. Do good with it to make up for our many mistakes.'

Molly took the gem in her shaky hands and then turned around and said to Amy, 'is this what you're looking for?'

Amy was too scared to reply so she nodded.

Will on the other hand had a score to even up with Henry, so he walked over to where Henry was crouched on the floor and snatched the magnifier from his pocket. 'I believe this is mine.'

Will held it up and noticed the shard of glass missing but within seconds of being back in Will's hand the glass returned to normal.

'You know Will, that's the second time I've seen that and I never tire of it,' said Hugh.

'It's pretty amazing,' agreed Will.

'Now Hillary and Henry... just so you know what happens from here. You will continue producing the ven-la-rocs and I will open your Hi House door, the same one that has been bolted for so long, where the nicbeings can come whenever they need them for their supplies. I will work out a way for the electricity to freely flow from here to any part of our planet that needs it.'

Max had something to say but was nervous so went over the Jack and whispered.

'What?' asked Jack.

Max whispered again.

'Tell them,' encouraged Jack.

Max was shy in this situation so Jack urged him again, 'Max has something to say.'

'While my paanic Pete has been building the overpass he installed hollow pipes that he found in the scrap heap at the twin Slava Slopes and put wiring in there so that if ever we got electricity the foundation would be there to use it.'

Molly had a smile from ear to ear as did Hillary and all the gang. The only one crying was Henry.

'How could you cry about that, Henry?'

'Molly, believe me, they are tears of joy.'

'That's a change of heart for you.'

'I know it is. I'm so sorry for all I've done. I don't know how long I have left but I promise I will do all I can to help not hinder and everything both Hillary and I have is yours and will be used for the good of Venus.'

Everyone cheered and Molly had tears in her eyes as she turned to Amy. 'Now I have an apology and it's known I'm not good at apologies. Amy I am so sorry I shook you as I did.'

'It's okay.'

'No Amy, it's not. Thank you for being good about it but if ever anyone touches you roughly again, you tell your maanic.'

'Hmmmm,' said Pat. 'While her maanic isn't here, I am her guardian and so Amy, please pay special attention to what Molly is telling you.'

'Thanks Pat,' Amy responded shyly as her face went red.

Will looked back up to where Zac had been and sensed he had escaped somehow but was determined to find out.

'Okay,' said Pat, 'shall we go and put the gem in where it belongs?'

Everyone cheered.

Jack and Max asked Hillary where the ven-la-rocs were while the team unbolted the front door and headed out. Henry slowly pushed himself up and Molly was the only one left.

'Molly, little libnic, how could I have done to you the things I have done.'

'Henry I've spent a long time trying to work that out since we used to get on so well and do so much together.'

'I don't know what got into me.'

'I don't either but I can assure you if it ever happens again I will be on your doorstep and putting it to rest, not leaving it so long.'

'I look forward to it.'

'You were always a better aquanic when you shared.'

'What's even funnier Molly is I really enjoy sharing.'

They had a giggle with each other and Henry put his arm around Molly and kissed her cheek.

'I hope that large cut on your cheek will leave a big scar and remind you of what not to be.'

'That glass came from the magnifier.'

'The magnifier?' Molly questioned.

'Yep. Will must be one special person.'

'I think all three of them are special; come and see what they've done for us.'

CHAPTER EIGHTEEN
MORE THAN
EXPECTED

Once back at the Date Wall Will and Amy had agreed that together they would click the last gem into place. They climbed the wall, one at each end, straddled it and met where the gem was missing.

'Everyone, can I have your attention.'

Many nicbeings had gathered, having been told over the two ways of what was about to happen.

'My friend Amy here, our dog Pat, and our friends Hugh and Reece and I would like to thank all you nicbeings for such a wonderful experience.'

'All right Will, we know you love us. Can you just click the gem in?'

Everyone laughed at Jack's impatience.

Together Amy and Will clicked the heart-shaped gem in place. Amy held up her ring and this time the beam of light went from the Date Wall to the twin Slava Slopes around to the twin Hot Spots and then to the Lava Hi House but there was nothing in the middle to connect them all.

'What's happened Will?'

'I don't know Ames but we better get to the little trickle of water that we left when last we were at the old sinkhole. There looks to be a problem.'

Will made an announcement that they would move to the sinkhole. Many nicbeings arrived there and stood around the circumference of it. The team along with Molly, Hillary, Henry, Jack, Max, Pete and Peg all stood side by side on one side. Jack and Max had bought trays of ven-la-rocs with them so they were distributed one per nicbeing. Pete handed Will a loud speaker.

'We need everyone on the count of three to throw your ven-la-rock to the centre where you see the trickle of water.'

There was a lot of noise as nicbeings spoke amongst themselves.

'I'm nervous Will. What will happen if this doesn't work?' asked Amy.

'When there's a Will there's a way,' was all he could add.

'That's not so helpful right about now.'
Pat was standing right there. 'Have faith Amy.'

'Okay. Ready? One, two, three.'

Thousands of ven-la-rocs were thrown in and this time within seconds a beautiful big consistently flowing fountain shot to the sky and kept going. The nicbeings cheered. They were so excited they ran through it, splashed each other, hugged each other and laughed. Even Hillary and Henry got in there.

Will ran in and out a few times then walked away to a nearby rock where he sat and looked to the sky to see Zac escaping in the CHAMJET. It was easy to identify because of the aqua blue colour and the bright silver nose. He wondered what Cyril's motive was.

Pete saw Will so he came over to him. 'Thank you, Will, for helping us.'

'No; thank you, Pete. This overpass is amazing and now you have the fountain, every time nicbeings use the overpass they can view the fountain.'

'And watch this Will.' Pete clicked his fingers and the overpass, the fountain and the four main structures lit up.

'Wow Pete! Venus looks amazing. How did you do it?'

'A lot of planning and a lot of hard work.'

Will laughed. 'Isn't it always the way.'

'Sure is. Thanks again Will,' said Pete as he bade him farewell and returned to his famnic.

The others now joined Will as they felt the bottles around their necks get really hot then a puff of pink smoke shot out and sure enough, there was CHAMJAN.

'Hello travellers, are we ready to go home?'

Will was not so excited. 'Guess so CHAMJAN.'

'What's up Will?'

'It appears your other half so to speak is transporting the enemy. Is that the reason he couldn't make it for us this time?'

'Will, you make it sound as though my services are not good enough.'

'Not at all CHAMJAN. You are great but I did see Zac take off in the CHAMJET.'

'It's another story for another time Will. Hop in.'

'What about Hugh and Reece?'

'We'll drop them on the way. Amy, you and Reece share and Will; you and Hugh.'

'Nah,' said Will, 'Reece you share with me.'

Hugh was delighted to be sharing with Amy in a small space. She turned to him. 'Don't get any ideas Hugh.'

'Be cool Amy, I won't.'

That one comment made her look at him in a different way.

'All right are we ready?'

'As ready as we'll ever be Pat.'

Pat let out a whistle and CHAMJAN took off. It was moments when they were back at the anyshapecart which was where it had been left and everyone made farewells. Then it was back to the original three.

'That was something else Will.'

'Sure was Amy. I don't think we'll forget it.'

'Ah Will?'

'Yes Pat.'

'Show me what came out of the mouths of the aquanic and libnic on the wall.'

'You really don't miss anything do you Pat.'

'Me either Will, I've been dying to ask but the right moment didn't come up.'

Will grabbed the mirrors from his pocket and leaned forward, giving one to Amy then showing the other one to Pat. As he went to sit back down the magnifier had edged out of his pocket and flown over the edge. He tried to catch it but it slipped through his fingers.

'The magnifier,' he screamed but CHAMJAN was moving way too fast and it was not in sight when he looked back.

Next Will heard himself puffing. *Keep running Will, you have to keep this clear ball turning and continue riding on this geyser.*

Amy was facing Will and she too was puffing like a steam train. She couldn't remember how long it had been since she'd run so fast.

Pat on the other hand had worked out how to keep his ball turning with less motion from him. He took it all in his stride.

'Ladies and gentlemen let's release our three stars!'

The geyser fountain underneath the three balls ceased as they were brought down and once back on the stage the plastic balls all opened as Will, Amy and Pat stepped out to a roaring crowd.

'What an amazing effort ladies and gentlemen, from our three stars, Will, Amy and Pat.'

Will and Amy held one another's hands and lifted them to the air while Pat lifted one of his paws. They cleared off the stage and wandered off to enjoy the rest of the show.

'What will I do without the magnifier?' mourned Will.

'I was wondering the same thing myself.'

'How will we get back to space Ames?'

'I don't know, but what I do know is that everything happens for a reason and it takes the team to make the dream.'

Amy and Will remembered that Pat could no longer speak to them but they noticed him smile at them as they walked through the rest of the exhibition chatting happily together.

Veer 2 Venus has now been
read
And we've now met Zac
Who fortunately is not dead
Move 2 Mars is the next
adventure to view
The magnifier's missing
What is Will going to do?